'That's Maori██████████. 'I'm not Maori.' But his friend Hemi, w█████████ him so much about the spirits of the Maori dead, who took the long path north to the farthest tip of New Zealand and then jumped off into the dark, that David began almost believing in spirits that could come back to the world if they had some specially urgent task to perform, ghosts that looked so like real people that no one would notice anything odd about them – except maybe that they never needed food or sleep.

David had another Maori friend, an old man whom he had found sheltering in a cave near the breeding colony of penguins he watched over, who had an unexpected understanding of David's difficult life at home, where his father scorned him, almost as if he were an unwelcome stranger instead of a son of the house. This old man told him still more stories of the spirits and of the sacred quest to find and cherish the club made of whalebone which the ancient hero Tarewai had lost and could not rest without.

Gradually, as he listened, David tumbled to it that these stories were being told to him for a purpose and that he, for a reason he had not yet understood, had an important part to play in the search that would bring peace to Tarewai and his heirs for ever.

Joan de Hamel was born in London and educated in England and Switzerland. She married and had five sons. The family went to New Zealand in 1955 and liked it so much the█████

An

X MARKS THE SPOT

JOAN DE HAMEL

Take the Long Path

With illustrations and maps by Gareth Floyd

Puffin Books

Puffin Books, Penguin Books Ltd, Harmondsworth, Middlesex, England
Viking Penguin Inc., 40 West 23rd Street, New York, New York 10010, U.S.A.
Penguin Books Australia Ltd, Ringwood, Victoria, Australia
Penguin Books Canada Ltd, 2801 John Street, Markham, Ontario, Canada L3R 1B4
Penguin Books (N.Z.) Ltd, 182–190 Wairau Road, Auckland 10, New Zealand

First published by Lutterworth Press 1978
Published in Puffin Books 1980
Reprinted 1987

Copyright © Joan de Hamel, 1978
All rights reserved

Made and printed in Great Britain by
Richard Clay Ltd, Bungay, Suffolk
Set in Monotype Bembo

Take the Long Path

Takahia atu ra
Te ara whanui
Ki te po tangotango
Ki te kawhangawhanga
Ki te kainga mo tatou
Te tangata

Take the long path
To the dense dark
To the waiting place
of spirits
To the final home
of man

TO MARY

Contents

'I don't,' cried David Regan categorically. 'I never do.'

'Well, I don't. Not always. Not usually. But some-times I do. I'm not too sure.'

David and his friend Hemi Waka were arguing. They stood on the shoulder of the hill where a creek oozed across the rough road, bypassing a blocked drain. The breeze from the Pacific swept their words away across the tussock paddocks.

'Ghost stories are kid stuff,' said David, pushing his fair straight hair out of his eyes. 'White sheets and rattling chains. They're stupid.'

'Not that sort of spook,' protested Hemi. 'More, well, spirits, you know. Returned spirits. Kind of lost souls coming back from the dark.'

'That's Maori legends,' said David. 'I'm not Maori.'

Hemi kicked a stone which bounced away from the steep paddock and landed in the bush that bordered the creek.

'Well, I am. And they're real beaut stories, they are.'

'Yes, but they're still *stories*. You just said it,' argued

David. 'Like that one about Tarewai we had in school today –'

Hemi was triumphant. 'Well, there you are! Maybe it's not all true. But Tarewai's a true person in history and he really lived round here and died in Fiordland and we copied that photograph of his greenstone club – she called it a "patu".'

Hemi wrenched a book out of his school bag and waved around an uneven drawing in green crayon of a weapon looking something like a stumpy cricket bat with two sharp edges. 'Who's ever heard of photographs of a ghost's belongings?'

'Wait on,' said David firmly. 'No one said Tarewai isn't true. I just don't believe his ghost is hovering around anywhere for people to see.'

'Not only seeing, Dave. Don't you ever have that feeling, a real creepy feeling that someone's around?'

'Could be some people do,' David conceded without answering the question. He turned to face the ocean. His eyes followed the thread of dark green bush to where the creek looped round a gorse patch and a stand of dead macrocarpa above the sands of Cray Beach.

Hemi saw where David was looking and had a sudden inspiration. 'So why haven't we ever been inside that old cottage down there? Because it's spooky. That's why.'

From up here you could not see the derelict building among the dead trees. It was just an old cottage built for a shepherd long ago, but David, in his heart, had to admit he had never been keen to investigate it on his own.

He said, 'I wouldn't mind going in!' rather more loudly than he intended. 'We'll do that sometime. Explore it together.'

'Like today?' suggested Hemi, with cunning. 'To-morrow?'

'Like hell!' David had to laugh. 'Dad's mustering today, and tomorrow's shearing.' He steered the conversation away from the subject of ghosts. 'Your Dad'll be over with the shearing gang and I'll be wagging school. Give out I'm sick or something.'

Hemi crammed his social studies book back into his school bag. 'All the kids have sickies for shearing and harvest,' he said. 'I'm taking one for fishing some day soon.'

'I'll come with you and we'll call in at the haunted house on the way. And, Hemi, keep track of things at school while I'm not there.'

'Okay.' Hemi started off back along the road towards his home. 'So long, Dave – see you.'

'See you, Hemi.'

David fixed the strap of his school bag so that he could carry it on his back and have both hands free. Then he climbed the fence on the left of the creek and ran down what was now a sheep track but which had once been the lane to the shepherd's cottage. He slowed down as he approached a tumbledown dry-stone wall among the grey roots of dead trees. Long ago a macrocarpa hedge had been planted to shelter the cottage, but it had grown too tall and the salt winds had killed it. Broken branches blocked off access to the decrepit old building. David stood on a fallen stone and peered at it through the criss-cross of dead twigs.

A lean-to had been built as a porch to the back door. The timber had rotted and the rusty iron roof had sagged and buckled. The chimney looked like a broken tooth. There was a kennel with the chain stretched out and old

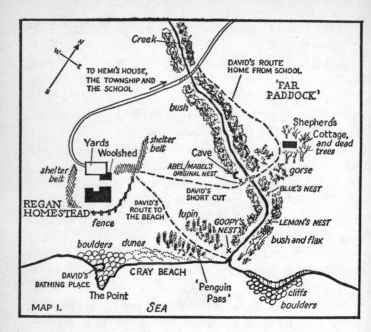

MAP 1.

bones on the bare ground, enough to feed the ghost of a
dog.

It was Hemi's talk that made David think of ghosts.
Now even he could imagine that the place seemed to be
waiting for something to happen, someone to come.
David shrugged off the ridiculous idea and followed the
wall round to where there was a small gap, blocked with
a coil of wire. From here he could see a lopsided verandah
crumbling with borer, a shut front door with a fanlight
over it and three windows. Two of these had broken
panes and were boarded up. The window to the right of
the front door, however, looked –

David gulped. Something had moved. Something he

had taken for dust or a reflection was moving before his eyes. Now there was nothing but darkness to be seen behind the glass; a moment before there had been a shape. A something.

David backed away. Some day, with Hemi, he would shout or make a noise and throw open the door and invade the house and laugh and play at Maori ghosts. But not alone. Not today. Today he had friends to visit and messages to be delivered.

He trotted off downhill along the path that led to the creek through the patch of heavy-scented gorse. The prickles scarcely scribbled on his bare legs because he knew every step of the way. He came along here several times a week after school to visit his private kingdom and its secretive inhabitants, the Yellow-Eyed Penguins.

He reached some solid stepping-stones which dated from the time the cottage had been built. David balanced on one of them and smiled as he recognized a penguin which was sitting firmly on its nest the other side of the creek, quite close to the path.

There is no difference between the plumage of a male and a female penguin but David could tell at a glance that this was the male, Abel. His breast feathers were tucked like an eiderdown over his egg, which was without doubt resting warmly on his fat pink feet. His feckless wife, Mabel, would have stood up by now, poised for departure. She simply did not have the know-how about incubating eggs. 'You ought to be ashamed of yourself, Mabel,' David had expostulated once, but it seemed she was not. She had even managed to let one egg roll out of the nest. David had found it, stone cold, and given it a modest funeral.

David's oldest friend in the whole penguin colony was Abel, so-called because he had a metal band marked **A B** round the top of one flipper. David had known and respected him for years. Poor Abel had lost his previous wife at the end of the last breeding season. Penguins normally pair for life and Abel had looked shabby and desolate, standing to moult all by himself on a heap of old feathers and quills. However, in spring he had reappeared with steel-blue-grey plumage, suffused with yellow on his head, and white breast shining like satin. And he had acquired a new wife, Mabel.

David failed to understand such a choice of partner or why the old nesting-place on the sheltered threshold of a small cave had been discarded in favour of this conspicuous spot far too near the creek for safety. Moreover, Abel seemed completely satisfied with his new home, a pathetic shallow scrape with a minimum of nesting material and a maximum of squalor. David, standing on the stepping-stone, savoured the odour of Mabel's lack of hygiene. Penguin droppings have a stench that can get you in the pit of your stomach but David was used to it and even thought of it as a friendly smell, a mixture of sweaty singlets, unwashed socks and sardine tins. To be honest, Mabel's residence smelt no worse than those of the other three families David had adopted, the Goopies, the Blues or the Lemons.

'Good day, Abel!' He spoke aloud to his friend. 'How'd you be?'

He walked quietly up to Abel and squatted down beside him. David had difficulty talking to people, except Hemi, but he loved to chat to the penguins, who listened with yellow-eyed astonishment and respect to his anecdotes and admonishments.

'Glad you're here, Abel. 'Fraid I need your special help for the next few days. I'll be shearing and I won't have time to come down and visit. I can trust you to see all goes well, can't I?'

Abel's pale yellow eyes flickered, the nictitating membrane swept back and forth like a camera shutter.

'It's the hatching that's worrying me. I know you'll manage your own chick and stop Mabel doing anything stupid. But Blue gets nervous and Lemon's not over-bright. And you know what Goopy's like. I really don't know how we'd manage without you, Abel.'

Abel seemed to enjoy lavish praise as much as David himself would have done if he had ever had any. Now he shuffled in apparent appreciation and shifted his weight. He half rose to his feet, arching his neck and touching the large once-white egg with the tip of his bill, which was yellow handsomely edged with orange. David thought he saw a star-shaped mark, like a pencil scribble, but the egg was so grubby it was hard to be sure and he had no intention of going nearer. A penguin had a right to privacy.

'Well, I'll be off now. Can you get a message up to the house if you need me? I'll be drafting this evening and the shearers come tomorrow. But I'll be down as soon as I can make it. Okay?'

Abel settled back on his egg, waggling his slate-blue behind.

'Regards to Mabel,' said David. Silly that bird might be but she was Abel's wife and the mother of his egg. 'So long.'

David stood up. A cloud of gorse scent drifted past, as though something had just shaken the heavy yellow spikes.

Immediately David was on the alert. He let his eyes travel inch by inch across the surrounding bank. Leaf by leaf he scrutinized the trees, stone by stone the boulders. It was not until he was facing uphill in the direction of the cave that he noticed anything unusual. The penguin path up to it had been well-trodden in previous years by Abel and his mate and offspring. This year, through disuse, it had begun to grow over. But now it was clear again, the way to the cave lay open.

David took his role as guardian of his private realm very seriously. He began to climb up to inspect the cave. Long ago the ground had slipped, leaving the rock face exposed and a shallow hole in the cliff behind. There was an overhang which made a kind of roof over the firm threshold of fallen topsoil, trampled flat. As he approached, David could see the traces of Abel's occupation in years gone by.

That was when the silence began. Thinking about it afterwards, David decided it had happened suddenly. One moment all was as usual and the next, sound stopped. No wind or creek or surf. Another step forward across the threshold of the cave, and sound returned; leaves rustled, water babbled, surf roared. David tried to be logical. There must be some natural cause for this. Perhaps for some reason the sound waves were deflected causing a ring of silence.

The cave looked the same as usual. Except – David scrutinized the shadows. Someone or something seemed to have been scuffling around in the sandy soil. For a moment David thought he sensed – not a presence: it was more like an absence – a void.

'Hemi's put ghosts on my brain,' David told himself as he backed out into the sunlight and slithered quickly back to the path.

'Nothing there,' he told Abel cheerfully.

Yet, irrationally, David no longer wanted to dally. Two of his adopted penguin families, the Blues and the Lemons, lived on the gorse-patch side of the creek. It no longer seemed necessary to visit them today. Nor even Goopy who lived under a fuchsia tree near the beach. In fact he made up his mind to go straight home.

He turned to Abel. 'I've just realized, I'm terribly late. Explain to the others, will you? So long, Abel.'

Usually David would follow the penguin path by the creek down past the fuchsia tree to the shore. From there he would climb up the dunes and through a tunnel, called Penguin Pass, which he cut every year through the wild lupin. Now, however, he was in such a hurry to get home that he left the path and fought his way straight through the undergrowth to take a short cut and emerge halfway up the paddock.

He hurried up towards the fence line and the shelter belt. Here for a moment he stopped and breathed deeply facing the ocean. On his right, just out of sight, lay the lonely homestead and the outbuildings of his father's small sheepholding. In the centre of the bay the pasture undulated down towards the lupins and the ever-shifting sand dunes. On his far left the other point of Cray Beach crouched over its boulder-strewn sands. David turned and looked inland. Here and there he could see the winding road leading over the volcanic hills of Otago peninsula to the farm. That was where, not long ago, he had assured Hemi that he never believed in ghosts. And there was the green thread of the bush, the golden mass of gorse and the black stand of dead trees. The cottage and the cave.

David put one foot on the prop of a strainer post and vaulted over the barbed wire.

From the yards behind the woolshed rose the din of bleating and barking. As he approached he could hear his father's angry voice swearing at the dogs.

At that moment David saw his mother scuttling towards the house. Her name was Joy, which David felt did not suit her. She had a big apron made of a sugar bag over her faded frock and was wearing David's gumboots. She looked hot and tired, wisps of fair hair were plastered across her shining forehead.

'Oh, Dave, thank goodness you're back early for once. Everything's gone wrong. I've been helping but now I've got to get the meal on. I really meant to cook ahead for tomorrow.'

David felt guilty. She thought he was back early. The truth was that he was so consistently late coming home from school that by now nobody missed him any more. He had to have some time to himself, to fool around with Hemi or visit his penguins. The moment he was home it was always 'Do this, do that,' from his father.

'Okay,' he said, 'I'll go.'

He slipped his school bag off his back and chucked it towards the house. His mother sighed and picked it up.

David scowled as he marched off to face the onslaught of his father's tongue and the stupidity of sheep.

Next morning, out at sea off Cray Beach, a white pointer shark snatched at a Yellow-Eyed Penguin just before dawn. The first bite took the bird's left leg clean off, but at that moment the dark cloud shape of a shoal of fish surged into view and the shark was away after them with a flick of its ugly tail.

The injured bird veered shorewards, swimming with flippers only and trailing blood. Now, struggling in the surf below its nesting place, it called feebly to its mate, which answered and came threshing through the flax, slithering down the grass, stumbling over the rocks in a helter-skelter to the rescue.

For nearly half an hour the injured penguin tried to leave the sea, urged by its mate which splashed noisily around, trampling the shallow water and wet sand with hefty feet. If one wave floated the injured bird up the shore, the next would roll it over and suck it back. Eventually it was easier to submit, to drift with the slack tide and give up the struggle.

The mate of the dying penguin reached a crisis of

despair and began to shriek, long harsh strident cries which made all other things pattering around in the half-dark stop in their tracks and crouch with fear.

David, in the homestead on the headland, woke up. The shrieks reached a crescendo. Then stopped. He propped himself up on an elbow. He had never heard a penguin call like that before. Something must be wrong. But what could he do? He lay down again. It was no use pretending he could hold the flipper of every penguin that was in trouble. Dozens of pairs lived among the boulders and flax of Cray Beach. There was no reason for that cry to have come from any of his four favourite families. Every year newly hatched chicks were taken by predators, tragedies happened, corpses were washed up by the sea.

David shoved his head under his pillow. Abel would be keeping an eye on things. Abel would cope. He'd said to Abel, 'I can trust you.' He'd said, 'Send a message if you need me.'

David re-emerged from under the pillow. Those screams weren't meant to be a message, were they?

No! He humped himself back into a comfortable position. That was nonsense. It was great to have Abel and the others as friends, but really and truly, well obviously birds can't understand human talk, don't send messages.

This line of thinking brought no comfort. He continued logically to the conclusion that Abel would *not* be keeping an eye on things and could *not* cope. Not really. Not at all.

'Okay, okay, hang on a minute, I'm coming,' cried David's thoughts to his penguin families.

In a few moments he was out of bed and dressed. His

sash window was open at the bottom and he dropped lightly on to the concrete path. In the half-darkness he avoided the clothes line, ducked away towards the fence. The dogs jangled their chains from behind the woolshed but did not bark, their hearing dulled by the night-long jostling and clamour of sheep and hungry lambs.

Soon he was careering full tilt down the damp paddock. Along the shore and out to sea on the reefs, the waves curled and sometimes caught the light from the eastern sky, gleaming like the silver thread inside a thermometer. David only saw the ground beneath his feet. He dived into the tunnel through the lupin – Penguin Pass.

As he emerged there came the repeated staccato call of a penguin close by. He stopped and listened. That would be Goopy under the tree fuchsia, summoning his mate from the sea. It was time to change guard duty at the nest.

'Everything's normal,' David told himself. 'No need to panic.' He stood still, getting his breath, surveying the beach. It was low tide, the surf tumbled gently. On a silver wave he could see a dark shape appear and disappear. Too big for a penguin. Twice the size – *two* penguins.

Here was something certainly very wrong. At this time of year, if one penguin was in the water, the mate ought to be on duty at the nest.

David peered into the silver and half-dark. Then he walked out across the sand and into the reflections and resolutely on into the ice-cold surf. He walked with numb legs in a semi-circle round behind the two birds like a dog shepherding sheep. One penguin dived and zigzagged away, then bobbed up, head and tail held high. The other penguin floated inert, lulled by the to-and-fro of the water. David splashed towards it, peered over it, struggled against an instinct not to touch and then scooped it up with both hands. It was heavy. The water ran off the stump of a leg, the claws of one foot, the dangling flippers. Round the top of one flipper gleamed a silver ring.

'Abel!' David stumbled towards the shore. 'Oh, Abel. I should've come quicker. I didn't realize. I'm sorry. I'm so terribly sorry.'

Now he was on the beach. He stooped and laid the dead penguin on the sand. With one finger he stroked the pale head. 'I promise, Abel, I'll help them.'

The mutilated body looked like a chewed-up bundle of feathers, old rags.

'Good-bye, Abel.'

Mabel reappeared from nowhere. She charged towards David, head down, swinging her heavy bill, flippers outspread to steady her hobgoblin gait. He stood up and advanced towards her, shooed with his arms. She hesitated, torn between her fear of David and her longing to rouse her mate. Eventually she turned and stumbled away up the beach. He followed, urging her on. When she found herself on the familiar penguin route she reacted to her maternal instinct and shambled clumsily up it towards her nest.

Numb with cold and grief, David began to dig a hole in the dry sand. He had hardly started when there came a low hissing sound from the sea. He glanced up to see a giant wave racing towards the shore. He knew these freak waves, had nearly been caught in one before. Run. That was all you could do.

He scrambled up a bank, threw himself into the lupin. The wave broke and rushed above high water mark to attack the dunes. Seconds later it collapsed, subsiding in the soft sand: then retreated, sucking back booty from the flotsam and jetsam of the shore and bearing away Abel's body for burial at sea.

David sprawled in the lupin. He had said 'I promise . . .' to Abel. But supposing Mabel went and deserted? The least he could do was to see if she had returned to the nest.

He stood up and set off uphill by the penguin trail beside the creek. A thrush was repeating a few tuning-up phrases. The dawn sky glowed across the bush. The shadows were violet as David emerged on the path near the stepping stones, below the cave.

Mabel was there all right, fussing around in a way he had seen other penguins behave when their eggs were hatching. What chance had a chick without a father? David's eyes pricked with tears.

Then stupid Mabel seemed to forget about her off-spring. She stumped on to the path, never noticing David, and craned her neck, trying to inspect, first with one eye, then the other, something which had caught her attention up near the cave.

David's mind immediately leapt to the most common dangers, a stoat or a dog. Well, that he could deal with. He rushed blindly up the bank. Suddenly a surge of silence broke over him like a wave, submerging him in quietness. He raised blurred eyes. For a moment of suspended time he thought he saw a man at the back of the cave. Was that a Maori face? The violet shadows moved, streaking the features with marks like the tattooing in the old days of Tarewai.

David rubbed his sleeve across his eyes, blinked and refocused with care. Nothing there. Or at least nothing visible. He stepped back out of silence into the hubbub of the dawn chorus.

Now David's only thought was to get home. He scrambled and ran by the short cut, through the bush. By the time he was climbing the fence he heard barking and shouts and realized with dismay that his father too had been up at dawn, to move the sheep.

He scampered down to the back door. Suddenly his mother appeared at the wash-house window. Her early-morning face gaped, looking the same colour as her nearly white nightdress. David made a dash round to his open window, clambered indoors and was under the coverlet before his mother came down the passage and opened his bedroom door.

'Where've you been? What's up?'

David wriggled. 'Nowhere. Nothing.'

'What if your Dad knew?'

'Don't tell.'

'That I won't,' said Joy. She looked at him uneasily. 'I'm getting a cuppa. I'll bring you one.'

Without waiting for an answer she went out, leaving the door ajar, and David could hear her old slippers flop-shuffling back to the kitchen.

3

David panted up and down behind the mob of sheep because his father was short of a huntaway dog and had not finished drafting the previous evening. Yellow dust rose from the hundreds of small hoof-beats and there was a turmoil of bleating from the frightened sheep and lambs as they were driven into the yards.

David's mind was not on his task. He dragged the gate shut behind the mob. If only he could shut out the guilty memory of how he had dallied in bed. And the sight of Abel with one leg bitten clean off.

David's father, Bob Regan, enormous and sweating, manipulated the pivoted race gate with one huge hand. Rapidly he swung the gate, left, right, right, left, separating the flock as the sheep dashed from the yards into single file along the narrow race; ewes to the left, lambs to the right. David was worrying now about the other penguin families which he had entrusted so casually to Abel's care. 'I could slip off at smoko time,' he thought. In his heart he knew that was impossible, since Bob Regan had an eye on everything that was happening.

'David!' roared Bob from the race gate, his voice gritty with dust and abuse. David saw him pointing impatiently at the lamb pen, and knew what was expected of him. Some of the ewes had managed to push by the race gate with their lambs. Grudgingly he mounted the fence and jumped from it on to the nearest ewe. With his thighs he clung to the ewe's heavy fleece and, with his feet just touching the ground to steady the bucking, he steered the creature to the fence by pulling its ears. In the past he had enjoyed this particular chore, kidding himself he was a rodeo rider. But not today. The heat was so oppressive. The smell of sheep nauseated him and anyway, he was getting too old for kids' play.

Here came Henare Waka – Henry Walker, Bob called him – the fleecie of the local Maori shearing gang. David was small for an eleven-year-old and not strong enough to lift a ewe, but Henare was broad and muscular, like most Maoris. He reminded David of the picture at school of Tarewai the warrior, with a feather cloak strung across his giant shoulders.

'I bet Hemi wishes he was here too,' said Henare as he bent over and picked up the ewe with a swing of his brown arms. 'Better than school, eh?'

David nodded but he did not really agree. Since he could not get away to the penguins, he felt he would rather laze at school with his friend Hemi than do this hard boring work in the heat and dust.

The big Maori gave him a friendly grin as he released the struggling ewe.

'We could do with you inside,' he suggested kindly. 'Take a spell out of the sun. I reckon there's thunder around.'

26

There was a shout from the shed. The shearers wanted more ewes in the catching-pens. Henare pushed back through the ewes and ran up the ramp. David followed him, looking sideways at his father and expecting to be called back. Bob was scowling at a line of black clouds on the southern horizon.

Inside the dark shed it was suffocatingly full of sheep and their acrid smell. Two shearers bent over their work, one on either side of the Cooper's Little Wonder, which clattered away, generating power for the shearing. The engine was knocking. Even David knew the men must have tried to pep it up. When Dad came in there would be words.

David drove more animals into the catching-pens, then picked up the broom to sweep the board. Henare was coping with a backlog of fleeces, quickly bundling them up and stacking them temporarily into a bin. The fat shearer, Wiremu, had just grabbed another ewe round the throat, making her stagger back on her hind legs before collapsing in an ungainly sitting position next to the stand. David thought of a shark snatching at a penguin. Wiremu held the ewe by one front leg, tucking her head under his elbow, pulled the trip cord, picked up the handpiece and away he went, shearing down the belly. Abel's belly had been torn by the shark's teeth.

The shearers kept their heads down, working fast. The thin man, Tepeni, finished the long blows to the tail on the last side of his ewe. As the fleece fell, he shoved the naked creature between his legs and out of the porthole into the small pen outside to await the tally.

'It's time for smoko. Where's the boss?'

A terrific rumble resounded from outside and David's

27

father appeared with thunder in his voice that echoed the thunder in the suddenly darkened sky.

'Blowing up a southerly,' he roared. 'I need help getting this mob under shelter.'

Wiremu finished his ewe, exchanged glances with Tepeni; they shrugged their shoulders, plucked at their black singlets, hitched up their tweed trousers and walked away. Not their job to drive sheep for a boss they disliked.

'Come on, David,' shouted Bob.

Henare had been about to follow the shearers. He hesitated, looking at David who had sat down the moment the shearers had stopped work.

'I'll give you a hand,' he said, 'that one's all in.'

'He'll last another ten minutes,' said Bob. 'Get on your feet, David. If Henry'll help bring in the lot I've just drafted, you pack the pens full to make room.'

David hitched himself off the bale and slouched off to do as he was told. As he finished, heavy rain clattered on the iron roof. David wriggled out of one of the portholes, startling the cold, newly shorn ewes outside, and made a dash for the house. He crossed the farmyard, ducked under the revolving clothes-line, and reached the back porch. There he kicked off his gumboots and shuffled with flipperlike socks into the kitchen.

'Take off those boots,' said his mother, without looking round. 'Go and get clean and dry.'

David turned on the wash-house tap, sloshed his hands and face and rubbed the grime off on the already grubby roller towel. He peeled off his wet shirt and dropped it on the floor, taking a dry one from the unironed washing-pile instead.

Then his mother did turn round, a pot of tea in her hand, a frown line between her pale grey eyes.

'Where's the other two? They can't work in this.'

'In the shed,' said David, 'fixing things up.'

'Isn't that like men? I get everything ready to take out there, then it rains and I put it out here, and now half of them don't come. And if I'd been five minutes late with the tea, I'd never've heard the end of it.'

The two shearers, already emptying their first cuppas and munching scones, slipped David sly looks of masculine complicity which he pretended not to notice, out of loyalty to his mother, though he was flattered to be included.

'Here's yours anyway, son,' she said, passing him his favourite big mug. David sat down heavily on a stool, cleared enough room for his plate on the untidy table, and began to eat his way through a pile of fresh-baked and ready-buttered scones. They were still in the basket that his mother had been going to carry out to the woolshed with the cups and a big billy of tea.

'How many still dry?' asked Tepeni.

'About a hundred and a half in the shed,' said David. He ran his left thumb over the familiar pattern on the mug. There were flowers twisted round an initial R for Regan.

Wiremu laughed. 'Another cuppla hours – we'll be away after dinner I reckon.'

Only a hundred and fifty to shear and four grown-ups to do it! David finished his mug of tea in a hurry, stood up and belched. His mother gave him one of her looks but could not say anything because the shearers had been doing likewise at regular intervals. David slid two more scones into his pockets and was out of the kitchen into the front hall as Joy turned back to the window over the sink where she stared at the scudding thunder clouds, her wrists trailing in greasy dishwater. Then he was through the front door, over the puddles along the path in his socks, ducking below the level of the wash-house window and into the back porch for his gumboots and parka without being seen. He forgot about being tired now he had his own way. He was off up to the shelter belt and the fence line, wrestling with his parka zip as he ran. Out of sight behind the trees, he stopped to put up his parka hood and fasten the domes.

A great gust blew savagely in from the south. David put down his head and battled downhill against the wind and rain sweeping in across the Pacific. In a couple of minutes he was partly sheltered by the dunes. The yellow lupin spikes, the scent washed out of them, tossed about scattering raindrops. A pipit got up from almost under his feet and was swept away downwind. David dived into Penguin Pass. On the far side he rushed for shelter under the tree fuchsia near the creek. This was Nest One where the Goopies lived. It had a tidy rim of pieces of flax and dry grass.

One Goopy was at home. David always called whichever penguin was there by the family name. Only Abel and Mabel had individual names.

'Gooday, Goopy. Twins hatched yet?'

Both Goopies, although house proud, had a permanent expression of stunned anxiety, as though someone had once dealt them a sharp tap on the head with an egg. It looked as if the yellow yolk had run backwards across their pale pates and congealed in a ring round the base of their skulls.

'But Abel,' remembered David, '*he* used to wear his yellow ring like a golden crown.'

Today Goopy was emitting a fizzling noise through his bill.

'No sense being nervous,' said David sternly, like the Plunket nurse at the baby clinic. 'They'll hatch soon enough. Worrying'll do no good to anyone.'

Goopy half stood up (David accepted this as a mark of respect) and then settled a grimy breast on the two eggs, flicking drips of rain off his tail.

Now David hesitated. Should he go straight up this side of the creek to Mabel or cross over and visit Blue and Lemon first? Perhaps it was the memory of the apparition in the purple shadows that influenced his decision. He hunched up against the onslaught of the rain and made a dart across the creek. From here he followed the white splodges on the penguin path up to Nest Two under a stunted ngaio tree. There crouched Lemon. A drop of rain ran down her bill and trembled on the tip as she peered forward.

'Your handkerchief, if you please,' said David sternly, and then stopped, delighted. Two very small bunches of grey fluff were balanced on her pink wrinkled fleshy feet. She flashed a look at David. 'Was it you?' she seemed to be accusing. 'Someone smashed my eggs and look what's turned up now!' Then she examined the chicks, with alternate eyes, touched them gently with her bill. They moved, so she hastily shuffled forwards and sat down on them.

'Congratulations, Lemon,' said David. 'Keep them well wrapped up. We don't want them catching chills in this weather, do we?'

David crawled out backwards, his knees and hands sticky with mud and penguin mess. He scrambled further

31

up the creek to the gloomy site of Blue's residence, crept in and peered cautiously into the darkness to find himself nose to bill with a hostile penguin peering out.

'Blue, you startled me. What a way to greet a visitor! Where are your manners?'

For the last fortnight, Blue – he or she – had been particularly friendly. One day David had spent nearly half an hour gently, gently moving his fist closer to the sitting bird, until he was stroking its throat. Blue had seemed mesmerized by the movement. Gradually, still caressing with his thumb, David had straightened his fingers under the brooding breast, lightly touching both eggs with his fingertips. Then slowly he had taken his hand away. He had done the same on every visit since that occasion. Blue positively seemed to enjoy the rhythmic caress. Today, however, David had hardly begun to reach out his arm, slow motion, before Blue stabbed wildly at his wrist. He managed not to flinch.

'Watch it, Blue. You're a bundle of nerves,' he told her, keeping absolutely still and seeing a meagre dot of blood ooze up on his wrist. 'We all have our anxieties,' he lectured, looking into her pale yellow eyes. 'We must keep our heads; self-control; all that.'

By now he was pulling slowly away, but Blue stood right up and aimed another blow at his arm. David parried this one on his parka sleeve and at the same time noticed a small hole in one of the eggs. David's voice changed. 'I do apologize,' he said in the honeyed accents of the local vicar. 'I realize I've not come at a convenient time. I'll call again in a few days, after the happy event.'

He got back on his heels and crawled out into the rain. Now he would visit Mabel: and put out of his mind that nonsense about apparitions. He glanced quickly towards the gorse and the cottage, then stumbled across the creek, which was foaming right over the stepping-stones. He caught sight at once of a ruffled penguin. That was Mabel all right, poised for departure. David stopped at the sight of her nest. It was nearly awash with creek water. And it was empty.

'No!' cried David out loud.

Off went Mabel, tripping as she scurried. Now she was on her stomach.

'Mabel!' he exclaimed. 'You can't just skiddaddle and leave it all to me! Where's it got to, the egg? The chick?'

Flippers going like paddles, Mabel slithered downhill through the mud to the ever-welcome refuge of the sea.

David began a grim search downstream along the edge of the creek. Would an egg have sunk? Would a baby penguin chick be able to swim, like a duckling? He explored further, finding new dams and backwaters, rapids and whirlpools. No egg, no chick. He got soaked.

At last he trudged back to the empty nest. Well, that was that. Would even Abel have prevented this disaster?

There was one direction in which he had not searched and that was uphill towards the cave. He stared up at it suspiciously through the slanting rain. Better check. Because of his promise to Abel. He climbed the slippery bank.

This time he was expecting the silence barrier. For a second or so the rain fell softly like snowflakes. Then it drummed again on the hood of his parka. He stepped into the cave and – stopped in his tracks.

There, sheltered by the overhang of the cave, was a shallow scoop in the sandy soil. In it sprawled a smoky black chick, its first down fuzzy like a crew cut. Rolls of baby fat showed through the fuzz. There was a white blob on the tip of the tiny black bill. The legs and feet might have been made of black wire.

'Wow!' exclaimed David, forgetting everything else in his elation. 'So you've shifted house, have you? Your Mum never let on.' He chattered on heedlessly to Abel's heir. 'Gave me a fright. Hey, is anything the matter, kid? You don't look too happy?'

The chick was kicking feebly. There were some wisps of flax in the scrape but David realized what was missing.

'She's forgotten your bedding. No mattress. Hang on, I'll fetch it and be right back.'

David slithered down to the old site so fast there was hardly time for any silence. Soon he was crossing the invisible barrier again, this time with his fingers stuck together with a mess of congealed penguin droppings from the crust round the previous nest. He rubbed one hand up the route.

'Just leaving instructions in case Mabel forgets where she's shifted to. Your Mum, well she's a bit, well, vague –'

He shook droppings lavishly into the hollow of the new nest, gently moving the chick from one side to the other.

'There you are,' he announced. 'All home comforts. A desirable residence. Wall-to-wall carpet.'

He pushed back his parka hood with one hand – gee what a pong!, cupped the other hand lovingly over the chick to give it the real home atmosphere.

'I promised your father –' he began. Then decided it was easier to be flippant. 'Smells like home now, doesn't it? You know, I can't think how Mabel came up with an idea like that. How'd she shift you – in your push-chair?'

34

Suddenly a man's voice came from the back of the cave.

'Well, perhaps it's time I explained. To tell the truth it was my idea. I'm responsible.'

David jumped to his feet and swung round. He found himself looking straight into the watchful face of an old Maori man who was peering out from the dark at the back of the cave.

'Don't be scared,' said the man, 'I didn't mean to scare you. I thought you'd better know how it came about. That's all.'

David stood and stared, embarrassed by his own silence yet unable to speak. There is nothing to say to someone who appears like a ghost when you have just been chatting out loud to a baby bird about carpets and push-chairs.

'I was going to come out when I first saw you,' went on the man, who spoke English with a lilt and a resonance which few pakeha New Zealanders achieve. 'Then you started yarning so I lay low.' He smiled and his brown face became deeply corrugated with wrinkles. He seemed not to notice David's silence. 'I hope you approve of this spot. I never thought to move the mucky bits. A nice clean nest, I thought.'

David nodded, opened his mouth to speak but no words came to mind.

The old man was beaming down at the chick. 'Penguins,' he went on. 'I remember when I was a boy –' He hesitated. 'That was a long time ago, but I couldn't stand by and watch that little fellow drown. My son – he went north – would there be these yellow-eyed ones up there? At any rate he used to watch the penguins down here. I'm glad boys still care.'

At last David could speak. 'Most don't. I don't tell.'

'Very wise,' said the old man. 'There are things you can tell and things best not told. Some things can't be explained.'

David thought, 'Too right! A lot of things just recently. And what are you doing on our property?' But he said nothing.

'I'm sheltering from the rain,' said the old man, as if in answer to the unspoken question. 'You know that old cottage up there? That's where I'm staying. But I'm not very nimble through the creek and all that gorse, so I thought I'd sit here till the rain let up.'

David stood there uneasily wiping his messy hands on the seat of his pants. In the cottage? How could anyone want to stay in that old ruin?

'It's not such a bad spot,' said the man.

Now David was examining the old Maori detail by detail. His clothes were a far cry from the feathered cloak of Tarewai the warrior. He wore a dark blue pinstriped suit that was frayed and shiny, a grubby waistcoat to match. A shirt with no collar revealed the top button of a vest.

'I'm not dressed for the rain,' agreed the man.

'No,' said David.

He noticed the brown fingers were engrained with earth and were fiddling with a small shovel. So that was who had disturbed the sand at the back of the cave.

'Just digging around,' explained the Maori. 'Something got lost. Something belonging to the family. It's family business. You could call it that.'

'I see,' said David. Then with an effort he spoke up on

behalf of Abel's wife and chick. 'I'm worried about – well, actually I call her Mabel – the parent one. I suppose you heard. She's nervous.'

'Mabel, is it?' said the old man. 'I'll be very careful. I promise that.'

'With the nest being moved and – and' – he was going to mention Abel but his voice was giving out – 'and things. She might desert.'

The chick sprawled, its down moving fractionally as it breathed.

'Mabel won't desert,' said the man, 'that's a promise.' How could he be so certain?

'Well, good-bye then,' said David.

'Ka kite ano,' said the Maori.

David backed downhill. For a moment the silence held him, then he was skidding away through the bush, his face stung by gusts of rain.

When David reached home he noticed the shearers' car had gone. He kicked off his boots and hung up his dripping parka in the back porch. Through the sound of water running off the roof into the tanks and the splash of overflowing gutters, he could hear his father's voice, the familiar rise and fall, relating the calamities of the day and the inefficiency of all Maoris – indeed of everyone and everything except himself.

David walked into the kitchen and hesitated, the raindrops running down his fringe and trickling off his cheeks like tears. His knees were red, his socks sodden.

'David!' exclaimed his father. 'And who gave you permission to slip off like that?'

David remained silent.

Joy rose hastily, taking a towel from the line stretched across the coal range.

'Oh, Bob, let the child get out of those wet things first,' she said. 'Look at him, soaked to the skin.' She hustled David out of the kitchen, pressing the towel into his hands. In his room David rubbed at his hair and fell to thinking about the old Maori, and about Abel and Mabel and the chick. He had so much to think about he forgot to change his clothes. It was not until he found himself shivering all over that he put on some dry things and went back to the kitchen. By then he was so cold that even kneeling by the range did not warm him. His teeth were chattering as he half listened to his father holding forth about the fall in wool prices with an edge of accusation in his voice as though the weather forecaster, the Maoris and his wife had connived to drop them on purpose.

4

Next day, Bob Regan was in a better mood.

'This breeze'll dry them,' he said to David after breakfast. The two of them stood on the woolshed ramp. The unshorn ewes on the slope of the hill looked like smoke against the grass. 'We'd better get cracking.'

He turned and in silence David followed him into the woolshed. The bins were overflowing with unskirted fleeces.

'If the weather holds, the men'll be back tomorrow. We'll see how much of this we can clear today.'

David nodded. Lucky shearers with the day off. However, he set to work with a broom while his father picked up a fleece and threw it over the table so that it landed fully spread, the edges hanging down. With deft fingers Bob plucked and pulled at the skirtings till the fleece was trim and the wool firm. Then he folded in the sides and rolled up the fleece from one end and passed it to David, who now stood in the sack ready fixed in the woolpress. When there were five fleeces in position and David was trampling down this bottom layer, there was the noise of an approaching car. David caught a glimpse of it through the open door, identified it succinctly.

'Waka's.'

Bob straightened his back. 'Henry Walker? Let's hope he's come to give a hand and not to go on about that block of land. I'll waste no more time on that.'

The sharpness in his voice annoyed David. His father never seemed to have a good word to say for any Maoris, he did not even have the courtesy to try to pronounce their names. But this was the first time David had heard land mentioned. He wondered which block was in dispute. The next moment he forgot his annoyance because he saw both doors of the car open and a boy jump out as well as a man.

'Hemi!' exclaimed David.

Bob, however, was immediately suspicious.

'Now what's up? Why's he brought that boy? I'm not going to pay a child wages.'

The big Maori and his son presented themselves.

'Morning, Bob,' said Henare Waka. 'Great drying weather. I reckoned you could do with a hand to get those fleeces baled before tomorrow.'

'Maybe,' said Bob, throwing another fleece and carrying on with his work.

'I've brought along Hemi,' went on Henare. 'I thought he could help around.'

'If he works, he works for free,' said Bob crisply, 'same as David here.'

'Hemi's not looking for payment,' said Henare. 'Maybe the boys'd like to push off together and I'll do David's share, and my own too.' He smiled at David and gave him the ghost of a wink.

Bob's face reddened. 'What David does is my decision, and I say David'll do a proper day's work. Just because your son's at the same school as mine doesn't mean they've a right to slack around together.'

For a moment David saw the scene as if it were a still from a film, his father's ugly red face and Hemi's mouth wide open with astonishment. Then Henare retriggered the action, holding out his arms towards the boys, and speaking with calm dignity.

'Our boys work and play together at school. I reckon they can do the same here. If you'd rather not, he'n me'll push off home and I'll not bother coming back to-morrow.'

David looked down and started trampling the fleece again. He knew that nothing was more important to his father than getting the shearing finished the next day. Sure enough, his father said in a conciliatory voice, 'We'll try him out then. Might be able to spare a few eggs for him to take home.'

In the lunch break the Wakas sat out in the sun eating the food they had brought with them. Joy gave cautious praise.

'Really nice of them to come. That'll make a big difference to you, and no bother to me, seeing they aren't expecting a meal.'

Bob grunted and filled his mouth untidily with salad. When he had finished and gone out, David stayed behind to give his mother a hand with the dishes.

'S'funny,' said David, vigorously rubbing a cup, 'Dad's really got it in for Maoris.'

His mother clattered the plates. 'He hasn't got it in for Maoris. You're imagining it.'

'*Mum*,' said David reproachfully. He juggled the cup on to its hook on the dresser. The crockery was at risk in this conversation.

His mother spoke in the jaunty tone which she always used when covering up for her husband. 'Well, there's been a spot of trouble lately over a few acres of land.'

David was interested. 'Oh yes, he said something this morning.'

'That'll be it. It's the far paddock, beyond the creek.'

David was even more interested. 'That's where that old cottage is.'

'That's the one. Your Dad bought it in good faith to get enough acreage for sheep, then one day along comes a Maori deputation and claims that block. Wanted it back; wouldn't pay; said it had been Maori land since before the pakeha came from overseas and called themselves New Zealanders. The thing was, when it was all gone into, the Maoris were right. It really is tribal land. Goodness knows how many of them share it. Dad had to resign his rights. No compensation of course.'

David said, 'First I've heard of it.'

'It happened years back when you were still in naps. But the Maoris have never done anything with that paddock. It's all gone to gorse. Your Dad could do with the extra land. So just recently he tried again – offered to clear the gorse and rent the grazing. They refused.'

David nodded. 'I get it. Dad'd feel kind of one down.'

Joy wrung out what she always called her 'dish clout', one of the few Yorkshire terms that remained from her childhood vocabulary. 'That's what I mean,' she said, 'he lost mana.'

David understood the implications of 'mana'. He also knew that his mother never used a Maori word when his father was within earshot. 'Lost face,' she would have said, not 'lost mana'.

'Oh well,' he mumbled indistinctly, 'back to slavery.' He shambled off.

In the woolshed everything went smoothly. Bob Regan

and Henare Waka dealt with the fleeces and worked the press, helped by the boys trampling the rolled-up fleeces. David stitched up the bales and Hemi marked them by brushing blacking through a stencil. Henare soaked off the old emery paper and fixed a new one. The boys swept up the skirtings and finally cleaned out the holding-pens. Everything was tidy. Bob was pleased, though unwilling to give much credit to the 'Walkers' as he called them. He grunted thanks and took Henare to the house to settle up. David and Hemi sprawled on a wool bale.

'Say, Hemi, you could tell me something,' said David. He tried to sound casual but had been planning what to say on and off all day. 'There's a very old Maori around. We were chatting. He forgot to tell me his name and now it's kind of awkward to ask.'

'What's he look like?' asked Hemi. 'There's several old guys.'

'This one's really old,' David said earnestly. 'He's got a stripy suit and a waistcoat, the old-fashioned sort.'

He hoped to hear Hemi name the man and tell some story about how he was always wandering around and turning up in unlikely places. But Hemi was frowning at a blister on his hand and picking at it.

'Maybe someone visiting,' he suggested. 'Funny though. I haven't heard and we mostly know everyone. I'll ask around.'

'No, forget it. Doesn't matter.' David was wishing he had not asked. Hemi might mention it to his father and word could travel back to Bob. Presumably the Maoris had a right to visit the cottage on a patch of tribal land, but the cave was not in that paddock. Anyone, especially a Maori, trespassing and digging on farm property would

43

get short shrift. 'Oh and I guess I'll be off school Monday too, Hemi. Longer perhaps.'

'Neat excuse,' Hemi said, and stood up. His father was walking over to the car, holding a bulging paper bag with care. Hemi had earned his eggs, but David suspected they were a gift from his mother rather than wages from his father.

5

The next couple of days saw the end of shearing. It had been an especially tough time for David who seemed to have caught a chill from the soaking on the day of the storm. The generator in the shearing shed had clanked and coughed, sounding as sick as David felt with his throbbing head and tight chest. He had carried on sweeping the board and keeping the pens full but had not found the energy to dash down through Penguin Pass to visit the nests or see if the old man was still around.

Now he had a reward: one free day at home before going back to school. David was pleased, but wished he had been allowed to go to Dunedin in the truck with his parents. Bob Regan was off to see the stock agents and Joy had long ago planned to go too for shopping. Now she was having second thoughts because of David.

'Are you coming or are you not?' demanded Bob. His wife was scurrying hither and thither in a state of indecision. Would David be all right if she left him? Ought she to stay at home?

'Course I'm all right,' groaned David, fiddling impatiently with his mug and scratching a thumbnail over the pattern.

'Come on then, get moving,' said Bob.

Joy was turning out a kitchen drawer in a panic search for the knitting-wool she wanted to match and simultaneously gabbling instructions about David's lunch and welfare. David got up and handed her the ball of wool which he had noticed on the mantelpiece.

'Right!' Bob opened the back door. 'We're away.'

'I haven't even done my hair. Where's my handbag?' David found her comb and her handbag. Bob ushered her outside and she scrambled up into the truck smoothing her untidy hair.

'You want your apron on in town, Mum?' asked David.

Joy gasped and began pulling at her apron, which tightened the knot. The truck left amidst fumes of exhaust and exasperation and a torrent of gravel and admonishment to David to be 'sensible'.

David sat down on the grass to recover. Why couldn't his mother make decisions and stick to them? Fuss, fuss. She was all fluster and impulses, and could do with some tidying up – yes, and a bit of preening too.

He knew exactly what he was going to do with his free time. To obey instructions he fetched a jersey. A batch of biscuits was cooling on a wire tray in the kitchen and he filled his pockets. On the table he noticed the ball of wool which had been left behind after all in the turmoil of the departure.

Soon he was lolloping off towards the bay, down Penguin Pass and out by the fuchsia tree and Nest One.

Goopy sprawled across the nest and stared at David, turning her head from side to side.

'Gooday, Goopy,' called David, then remembered the Maori might be around and said no more aloud. He knelt down and saw her breast feathers heave. A small bright-eyed dark head popped out, then disappeared. A moment later several black feet emerged and were withdrawn.

'Congratulations, Goopy! Told you it'd come right, didn't I?' He hoped she could hear what he said to her inside his head.

The twins were exercising vigorously in the dark of their downy nursery. 'Gee, it must be stuffy,' thought David and imagined himself living inside an eiderdown. Better than cramped up inside an egg, though.

He crossed the creek, which was back to its normal modest width, and made for Lemon's stunted ngaio. The twins had grown from grey-black babies to dark brown toddlers. Lemon was endeavouring to brood them, but they were old enough to protest in reedy voices. As a foot or a flipper wriggled out from under her breast, she moved and sat down in a different position, which gave the other chick a chance to escape from under her tail. Lemon was completely non-plussed but looked very healthy, her cheek feathers tinged with pink.

David climbed up to Blue's dark territory. The chicks were smaller than Lemon's, larger than Goopy's. Blue did not seem to have regained her gentle character, but stared coldly at David with pale, unfriendly eyes. He had hoped to try caressing her again but decided against it.

He turned and re-crossed the creek, using the stepping-stones. The penguin track up to the cave was splodged with white messes and David's spirits rose. This meant the track was in use. Mabel must be feeding her chick.

He had forgotten about the silence thing. It smothered him like a moment's surge of cotton wool. Then there he

47

was on the threshold of the cave, with Mabel on her nest at his feet and the old man sitting in a patch of sunlight on a heap of newly-dug sandy earth.

'Haere mai. Haere mai. Haere mai.'

David had been taught by his mother that the correct answer to this greeting was 'Kia ora' and indeed he did say it, but self-consciously with a pakeha accent. He was surprised that Mabel had not made her usual exit. Her flanks heaved. The chick was very much alive.

'I was wondering where you'd got to,' said the Maori. 'Not like Young Tama to forget his penguins, I thought.'

'Shearing,' explained David, scuffling the sand with his toe. 'Why'd you call me that, Young What-you-said?' He felt he could ask because the man looked pleased to see him and anxious to chat.

'It's just a Maori word for a young lad. I used to call my son Tama. You remind me of him, you and your penguins. I've been thinking of you as Young Tama.'

David was slowly trying to remember.

'Mum used to call me Tammy. As a nickname. Ages ago, that was.'

The chick's head had appeared from under Mabel's flipper. She shifted and it disappeared.

'And your father called you that too?'

'No.' David felt safer asking than answering questions. 'What's your name?'

'I've been called a lot of names in my time.' He meant it as a joke but David forgot to smile. 'So you can call me what you like,' went on the man, determined to be friendly. 'When I was a lad they called me Tama too.'

'Old Tama,' decided David suddenly, 'if I'm Young Tama, you're Old Tama.'

'That's a bit of a contradiction, an old young boy. I've never been called that before.'

David shrugged. Mabel was suddenly almost levered to her feet by the chick making a stupendous bid for fresh air. The old man continued talking. 'Fair's fair, though. You've never been called Young Tama before either. So that's all right. Old Tama. That's me.'

The chick had now escaped from beneath the startled Mabel. David did wish the old guy would just stay quiet while he watched this domestic scene. He remembered the biscuits in his pocket. Perhaps eating would stop talking. He pulled out a handful of broken pieces.

'Mum just made these,' he said. 'Like a snack? I'm having one.'

'Thank you, no. No food for me. I'll tell you one thing. Mabel's having trouble keeping that chick filled up.'

Mabel did indeed look harassed. Her plumage was grubby and ruffled. The chick, however, was as neat as a pin and strong. It teetered bravely up on its two black feet, leaning forwards so that the tips of both pink-brown flippers rested on the ground. It screwed its neck round to look at David, rocked awkwardly and collapsed on its chest.

'I'll tell you something else,' said the Maori. 'Mabel's looking after that chick single-handed. Single-flippered I should say.'

'I know,' said David. 'A shark got her mate.' Again he felt the thud of guilt.

'She's still grieving for him, do you think?'

'Not she. Not Mabel,' scoffed David, suddenly finding words to express what he felt about Abel's feckless wife. 'She's the forgetful type, a flibberty-jibbet, here there and any old where. She even lost one of her own eggs. Though that's turned out for the best. Two chicks'd never survive with a mother like her.'

'Now that's a hard thing to say,' said the Maori. 'Poor Mabel! She's caring for that one all right. She leaves it a bare two or three hours to fetch food and then she must give it all she's found. Look how thin she is and how well the chick looks.'

David examined Mabel's angular breastbone, protruding shoulder-blades and shabby plumage, very different from the sleek appearance of the other penguins.

'Maybe you're right. It's just she was always changing her mind, hopping on and off the eggs.'

'She's caring for it all right now,' repeated the man. 'Things'll be tough for her as it grows bigger. It'll need more food. She'll just have to leave it for longer and longer.'

'That's a worry too,' said David. He was beginning to enjoy Old Tama's company, now they were talking about Mabel. 'I've seen it before. There's too many things that'll harm a young chick that's not guarded. Chicks aren't left on their own till about Christmas usually.'

Old Tama sighed. 'You talk just like my boy used to,' he told David. 'You remind me of him. He was forever disappearing off down to the penguins. Of course, you're so fair and he was dark, but you've got the brown eyes.'

David had to smile inside himself at being told he looked like a Maori boy. What would Dad say to that?

The old man was going on about his son. 'He went away suddenly to Auckland. It was because he went suddenly that I never told him about the family business I mentioned to you. He sent an address, but when I tried to find him, he'd moved on.' Old Tama sighed deeply. 'At any rate,' he added, 'I know where he is now.'

'Why don't you write?'

'Because they don't run a mail service there.' The man paused, sighed again. 'Not to the home of the ancestors.'

David hesitated awkwardly. 'He's – you mean he's dead?'

'That's it. If you want to come back from that place, you have to set your mind to it before you take the long path. Well now, he had no reason to do that because I'd never told him the Oha.'

'The Oha?'

'The family business.'

David put the handful of biscuit pieces back in his pocket. Somehow he no longer felt like eating. He did not care for the way this old man talked, as though death were a pre-planned business trip, from which people could return or not as they chose, merely a temporary or permanent change of address.

'I see,' he said at last. He longed to go home. Against his will he found himself putting another question.

'What was it you didn't tell him?'

Old Tama smiled as though that question was exactly the one he had wanted to hear.

'Well, I don't mind telling you if you like a bit of a yarn. My boy liked a yarn. You do remind me of him, for all your hair's so fair and your skin so white. It must be those brown eyes of yours.'

David was embarrassed and sat down. There was clearly no escape from hearing the story but he need not listen very carefully. He could watch the chick which was now half under Mabel's flipper again.

Old Tama was leaning back against the edge of the cave, his blotchy fingers folded across his waistcoat. The veins of his hands were like knotted hammock string. He shut his eyes and began his tale.

'Long ago there lived a warrior in these parts called Tarewai –'

Tarewai! David was listening after all.

'– he was a great fighter and a great leader. Being great, now that, Young Tama, you know that can set a man apart from other people. At any rate people feared Tarewai more than they loved him. But there was a boy, quite a bit younger than himself, who did him a great service and became a great friend. That boy was my ancestor.'

'I heard the start of a story about Tarewai at school,' said David, 'but I been away since. We did a picture of his greenstone club.'

Old Tama drew in his breath. 'Now we're getting somewhere. Because before he had the greenstone one – mere pounamu – he had a patu paraoa, a whalebone patu. He'd made it himself when he was a lad.'

'At school they told us about this place in Fiordland –'

The old man's eyes were open now. 'Young Tama!' He almost shouted it. Mabel hastily sat down right on top of her chick as if to block its ears. 'Just forget what they said at school. They were starting at the end, not the beginning. I'll tell my yarn in my own way. Stop interrupting!'

David was growled at more often for his silences than for his interruptions.

'Sorry,' he said, 'please go on.'

Old Tama eased himself a little nearer Mabel's nest.

Strangely she seemed not in the least disturbed to have him so close, though she had always been nervous of David. Occasionally as he told the tale, Old Tama caressed her gently.

'Tarewai. Well now, Tarewai, he came from the north and built Pukekura Pa. That was the name of a village which he fortified later. The remains of it are on the tip of this peninsula here, where the Royal Albatrosses nest at Taiaroa Head. You know the place?'

'Yeah. I been there.'

'That was Tarewai's base camp, as you might say. His sworn enemies were the local residents, the Kati Mamoe Tribe of Papanui Pa. That's near Cape Saunders, the other side of the inlet.'

David nodded. He knew the area.

'At any rate, one day, so the tale goes –' Old Tama's voice took on a new note as he related the traditional story. 'Tarewai and some of his warriors slip secretly out of their pa and go to spy on the Kati Mamoe fortifications, Tarewai leading the way. And suddenly there's shouting and he turns round and what does he see?'

David's imagination quickened. In his mind's eye he saw men fighting and killing. 'What was it?'

'His warriors have been ambushed by the Kati Mamoe spies, and the next moment, Tarewai himself is captured. Not without some trouble, I might add. It takes four Kati Mamoe warriors to hold him on the ground on his back. There he lies with outstretched limbs while two men wrestle with his arms and two more try to hold down his legs. A fifth man steals the weapon that is tucked into his waistband.'

'His weapon?' breathed David.

The old man nodded. 'With his own whalebone patu,' he continued, and now he was half chanting the story which he evidently knew by heart, 'and with sharp stones, they begin to cut him open to take out his heart. The chief of the spies mocks him. "With thine own patu . . ." '

David found his imagination drifting as he listened to the chant. He could see Tarewai stretched out, blood everywhere, someone bending and hacking.

Old Tama paused. With one thick finger he touched the downy head of Mabel's chick, which had managed to emerge again.

'Go on,' said David. 'What happens?'

Old Tama took up the sing-song chant again. 'It happens that the Kati Mamoe lookout notices strangers approaching and he cries out a warning. The butchers' attention is taken for a moment as they wonder if these intruders are friend or foe.' Now Old Tama was stroking Mabel who was lolling on her side.

'Tarewai, who has been lying quiet and still, feigning death, now ceases his pretence. Clutching his wound – for his entrails are already bulging through the gashes – he leaps to his feet and flees from his captors. Into the bush he speeds and with failing strength, struggles up the forest-covered slopes of Hereweka.' Old Tama broke off. 'That's what we'd call Harbour Cone, above Portobello. Quite a distance that.'

David nodded, willing himself to see pictures in his head. He closed his eyes. For a moment the tattooed face of a Maori Chief floated into focus. Tears and blood ran down across the blue-black whorls that spanned his cheekbones and emphasized his broad nostrils and firm chin.

'What did he do then?' asked David.

'He wept for humiliation and for his whalebone patu,' said Old Tama. 'He'd carved it himself and loved it dearly, and he vowed that one day he'd get it back.'

'How did he recover from his wounds?'

'A boy not much older than you, this boy, my ancestor, found him.'

'Tell me, go on.'

The old man shook his head. 'It'd take too long. Another day.' He suddenly looked very old indeed.

David knew he was being dismissed.

'I'd better go. Mum left lunch out. Have you got yours?'

'You don't have an appetite when you're old like me. Not like a lad your age.'

David stood up. 'Well, thanks for the story. I'll come again and hear the rest. And thanks for keeping an eye on Mabel and the chick.'

'You're welcome any time,' said Old Tama. 'I'm always up at dawn. And I won't let anything harm those two,' he said. 'I always keep my promises. That's why I'm here to see about the Oha.'

That word again. David let it pass for the second time. 'Good-bye,' he said.

'Ka kite ano.'

All the way up the hill David heard the rhythm of that phrase and at the back of his mind beat the other word, Oha, Oha, Oha. He wondered what exactly Oha could signify.

When Bob and Joy arrived home in the middle of the afternoon David was lying on the couch reading and looking as though he had been resting all day. The shopping trip had been a success in spite of not having the knitting-wool to be matched. He was hearing about it when there was a tap at the door and Hemi's face appeared.

'Hullo, Mrs Regan. Hi, David. I just walked over the hills to see how David was. Dad said he went crook during the shearing.'

'Hemi, that's very nice of you,' said Joy, before David could even say 'Hi'. 'I never realized that was you we passed.'

David detected the false note in her voice which meant she was lying. He also noticed her glance quickly out of the window to see where Bob was, as she added brightly, 'You should've flagged us down for a lift.'

David chipped in. 'Can Hemi and me go and fish in one of the pools?'

Joy hesitated. He could see her thinking, 'That'll keep Hemi out from under Bob's feet.'

'All right,' she said, 'but don't be long, take it easy. David's not too fit. Would you like a lemon drink, Hemi? You've had a long walk.'

Hemi accepted, and David's mug was filled too.

'I got a mug a bit like that,' said Hemi, 'with an H on it. Why's yours got R for Regan instead of D for David?'

'Oh I dunno, I've never thought. R's all right.'

Joy said, 'I'll give you some raw meat for bait.'

The boys set off at a demure pace. They reached the end of the bay furthest from the creek. Here the sand was always shifting and sea currents scarred the shallows into potholes. Sometimes the volcanic rocks were hidden under sand by the wind. Today they were swept bare as bones and they gleamed pumice white in the late afternoon sun. The boys pulled off their sandals.

'Let's go right out on the point,' cried Hemi, looking at the fingertip of rock that jutted into the sea at the end of the arm of the bay.

'Don't be daft,' said David. 'You know what the sea's like round here. People get swept off by freak waves and they're smashed against the rocks or eaten up by white pointer sharks.'

'Oh are they?' laughed Hemi, disbelieving.

'They are too,' shouted David. 'The penguins get eaten and slashed. I've seen a white pointer. It was in shallow water. Over there.'

'Don't you swim?' asked Hemi.

David began to race over the rocks. 'Come on. I'll show you where I swim. It's a beaut spot. No undertow and no currents.'

At the foot of the headland he stopped and pointed at a pool that lay in a cleft between the rocks. The sea flooded in at high tide, but the pool was landlocked when the tide was low, as it was now.

'Terrific,' cried Hemi, dragging off his clothes. 'You coming in?'

David hesitated. He knew what his mother would say about his chest and catching chills. But on an afternoon like this he would be dry before he got home, and he did not want Hemi to think he fussed about his health or was under his mother's thumb. He quickly undressed and followed Hemi into the pool.

Hemi was a really good swimmer. David swam well, but Hemi was like a seal, diving and twisting, then lolling about effortlessly on the surface, then disappearing and coming up underneath David.

At last they pulled themselves out of the water and lay on the prickly rocks to dry off. A slow thought formed in David's head.

'Hemi, do you know many Maori words?'

Hemi rolled over. 'Me? Not me. My grandmother does though. Karani we call her. She can talk Maori.'

'You wouldn't know what "Oha" means?'

'Oha?' repeated Hemi. 'Wait on. Oha. That comes at the end of some of the stories Karani tells. The Oha is fulfilled and then there is a big feast.'

'But what's it mean exactly?'

'I dunno. I could ask Karani.'

'Would it mean some sort of family business?'

Hemi's face lit up. 'That's it. Well, I think so. In the old days the Chief made last requests on his deathbed.' Hemi made his voice quaver. ' "Give my weapons to my son. Avenge the death of our warriors." Then he died and took the long path. That sort of thing. The tribe had to do what he said. Lots of revenge and massacres and whatnot, followed by a big feast. Something like that.'

David frowned. 'I see. Like making your Will. People promised to do what you asked. Did they always keep the promise?'

'I guess so,' said Hemi. 'I'll ask Karani if you like. Hey, let's dress now and start fishing.'

After the rushing around and the swim David was tired. 'It's a bit late,' he mumbled, starting to pull on his clothes.

'How about shellfish then?' suggested Hemi, dressing quickly. 'At home we love mussels.'

The boys began to look around the pools. Hemi soon went ahead and David lay down again and gazed into a small deep pool, staring through the reflection of the sky to the sandy bottom. Fleshy pink sea-tulips with stems like rope and undulating crimson anemones clung to the rock edges among the limpets and the bunches of grey mussels and the chitons in their jointed armour. There were two big flat yellow sea-slugs and some spiral white worms. Suddenly a shoal of tiny fish flashed across, electric blue and silver. David said nothing. He did not want to catch anything as tiny as that. He put one finger into the water and watched ripples expanding and other ripples contracting in rings with kaleidoscopic variations.

'Come on out here,' shouted Hemi. 'Give us a hand.'

David looked up and frowned. Hemi was out along the point hanging over the edge breaking off mussels. Black-backed gulls had appeared, squawking at the sight of smashed shells and at a rival group of red-billed gulls.

'Stupid idiot!' thought David. Slowly he stepped from

rock to rock towards Hemi. The ocean rumbled peacefully, scarcely wrinkling its surface as it slept.

'Look at all those,' shouted Hemi. 'Here, help me make a bag out of my skivvy.'

David did not answer but squatted beside Hemi and went on rather obviously watching the sea. Hemi gave him a sideways look, sighed, pulled off his skivvy, and began piling mussels inside it. David looked out beyond the turquoise depths of a deeply scarred hole to where the bull kelp twisted and turned with the to-and-fro of the sea. The whirls and fronds widened, tightened, relaxed, writhing like octopus arms. From time to time cloud shadows swept across the dazzling ocean or a ragged company of shags flew urgently past, like housewives rushing to a bargain sale, and passing other groups hurrying equally urgently in the opposite direction. In the far distance mollymawks glided and dipped, black, then white as they banked above the horizon and wheeled round to glide low over the far-off waves.

Hemi waved his arms at a gull which had alighted with exquisite precision on the mussel pile, theft in its shrewd red eye. 'You gotta hope!' he yelled.

David turned to look. The gull flapped out of reach and stood sentinel nearby. Then suddenly it rose vertically in the air. It had seen what both boys had missed – a huge wave racing towards them.

Just in time, David turned back. 'Run, Hemi!' he screamed.

Hemi tried to gather up his skivvy full of mussels, but it was heavy and he dropped it.

'Leave it,' cried David. 'Quick!'

Both boys fled, over the spiky barnacles and lava they

leapt and stumbled towards safety. The wave had broken. Now the spray caught them up. There was a hissing as the water rushed, creaming and foaming, at their heels. Hemi tried to run faster but David grabbed him by the arm and flung himself and his friend down behind a rock pinnacle.

'Hang on,' he gasped. And then they were both engulfed.

Through a green murky window David discerned streaks of seaweed and bubbles rushing towards the shore with stones and sand scoured up by the force of the wave. There was no moment in which to take a breath. Now the wave retreated into the sea, sucking and pulling as it travelled. Stones and boulders came rumbling back against the boys who were flattened to their sheltering pinnacle. Kelp ropes entwined them. 'I can't – I'll burst,' David screamed inside himself as sand thickened the water and sea foam frothed up in a lather of fury. Then suddenly, it had gone and the boys' heads were out in the bright air.

Clinging to the rock, half throttled with kelp, bruised and cut all over, David and Hemi looked fearfully at each other, and out at the now mild ocean. Without a word, both struggled to their feet, climbed over the barricade of loose stones and slippery weed. Silently they headed uphill for home.

Halfway up the hillside David said, 'I lost my sandals.'

Hemi nodded. 'Mine've gone too. And my skivvy. Can't be helped.'

They went on climbing. When they reached the fence they both flattened themselves and went under it instead of climbing the strainer post and jumping over. All the

61

bounce seemed to have been washed out of them. At the shelter belt, Hemi stopped for a moment and announced to David:

'You saved my life.' He wiped a trickle of blood out of one eye.

'You're joking,' said David. 'We both clung on to that spiky rock.'

'I wouldn't 've if you hadn't made me. I was trying to run for it. I wouldn't 've had a chance.'

David shrugged. 'We've got to get dry. There'll be trouble. Come on,' he said.

Bob Regan was in the yard. He must have been on the cliff and seen what had happened. Fear and relief had sharpened his tongue. Now his temper got out of hand. David, his power of speech frozen, tried not to listen. Everything, according to Bob, was Hemi's fault because he had come over without being invited.

Hemi began to say he was sorry to have offended, but when Bob interrupted, calling him a stupid hori, Hemi turned on his heel with dignity and limped off up the long twisting road, back over the hill to his home. David was sent indoors and patched up and then told to go to bed. Whether this was a punishment by his father or a safety precaution by his mother he did not know. He heard both their voices raised in argument as he dropped asleep.

7

'Why aren't you back at school?' demanded Bob, fitting thick rectangles of cheese across his bread at lunchtime next day.

David gripped his mug and stared at the R because he could not look his father in the eye. He knew he was fit again and none the worse for yesterday's bruises. But when Joy had given him a quick scrutiny that morning, he had managed to look battered and frail and scrounge one more day off school.

'Mum said tomorrow. It's such a long walk.'

His father slapped his hand on the table with so much vehemence that all the cups and teaspoons rattled. 'Such a long walk,' he mimicked in a namby-pamby voice. 'That wouldn't have carried any weight when I was a boy your age in Dublin. Why won't you toughen up?'

David was stung to anger, but his vocabulary could not rise to the occasion. He turned away his head, rejecting Bob's remarks.

Bob was irritated as usual by David's role of noncombatant. 'It's your mother's fault, she's too soft.'

Words rushed into David's mouth to defend his mother. 'Mum's all right. She's not soft. And not hard either.' He was terrified by his own daring in answering back. 'She doesn't want me hard.' Under his breath he added, 'Like you.'

Bob heard and shouted back, 'Not much chance of

that, I'd say. Some day soon you need to hear some home truths.' He nearly choked over his bread and cheese, then, grabbing a knife, hacked off a chunk of fruit cake, and strode out of the kitchen, annihilating the cake between his jaws. David shoved the remains of the cake into a paper bag. He was off to his penguins before his father got at him again and found him jobs around the farm. If, as he hoped, the old Maori was still there, David wanted to warn him not to get caught trespassing by Bob Regan.

Ten minutes later, in the safety of his own kingdom beyond Penguin Pass, David found Goopy's chicks asleep, their very breathing being supervised by an authoritarian parent.

Across the creek Lemon was disciplining one of the gawky chicks. A speck of khaki mud was lodged on its black-brown breast and Lemon's huge pink and orange bill was nibbling savagely at the dirt. Tufts like black thistledown floated away in the breeze. At Blue's nest the brats were also suffering from acute parent trouble. Blue was standing up trampling on them with heavy feet, trying to keep them out of David's sight. Adults were harsh. David turned away, full of sympathy for the young.

The approach to the cave had changed. On one side, well back from the penguin track leading up from near the stepping-stones, were heaps of freshly dug earth. The old Maori had been making progress with his excavations and had neatly placed the spoil where it did not change Mabel's access to her nest. David climbed up and pushed past the nothingness to see how things were getting on.

By the nest itself Mabel was preening. 'About time too,' thought David, watching her intent on a very tricky area over her breastbone which involved stretching her neck and then tucking down her bill at an acute angle. The chick stood at her side, comfortably rotund and placid. The old man was right. For all Mabel's shortcomings there was nothing wrong with her offspring, so far.

From the very back of the cave came the now familiar welcome. 'Haere mai. Haere mai. Haere mai.'

'Kia ora. Kia ora. Kia ora,' answered David.

This time he spoke the words naturally, like a Maori.

The old man emerged from a shallow trench which exposed the base of the cliff, brushing his earthy hands on the seat of his trousers exactly as David always did.

'I can't stay long,' said David. 'How's it going, the dig? Have you found anything?'

Old Tama held out a rusty tin and chuckled. 'Well, there's these indigestion tablets. I suppose those cannibals got terrible stomach ache. And over there I've put the usual fish and bird bones and lots of pipi shells.'

'No artifacts?' asked David.

'No. But proof that people have used the cave for shelter.'

David examined the pile of frail remains, fingering them as he tried to find suitable words for his message.

'Old Tama, there's something I've got to tell you. Warn you, in a way. About my father. Dad doesn't – well, he isn't – the thing is, don't let him catch you here.'

The old man raised his eyebrows. His wrinkled forehead looked like brown plough furrows.

'Thank you for the warning. It'll be all right though. I'm within my rights because that's Maori land where the cottage is.'

'The cave's not in that block.'

The Maori pursed his lips. 'I don't think he'll find me,' he said. 'But even the cave's on the track to the beach, a right-of-way.'

David did not understand laws of access. All he knew was that his father would object.

'That's okay then,' he said and changed the subject. 'Tell you what, I've learnt something I didn't quite get before. What "Oha" means. This digging you're doing, it's something your father wanted you to do, isn't it? His last wish?'

'That's about it, Young Tama, except it wasn't just my father's wish. Our family Oha dates back two hundred years or so. Each generation our people've tried to fulfil it. They've all failed and now with my son gone, well, it's up to me because I'm the sort that keeps a promise.'

'I know that's true,' said David, 'you've really kept your promise about Mabel and keeping an eye on the chick.' He smiled indulgently at the corpulent youngster. Its down was so thick that the general effect was of a grey-brown tea-cosy.

'Mabel's work entirely,' said Old Tama. 'You should see how her crop's bulging when she comes up from the sea. She gives it all to him. And now,' he hurried on, 'shall I go on with that story? I'd like you to understand what I'm at. I've a good reason for being here.'

David agreed eagerly and the two Tamas, young and old, sat down side by side.

'Where exactly was I?'

'The boy was finding Tarewai.'

'Ah yes. That was it. On Harbour Cone. The first thing the boy did was to fetch him water – at any rate, I think so – and then sea water too probably, in a kelp gourd, to wash the wound.' His voice gradually settled back into the story-telling tone.

'The salt water bites like a spider, but the bleeding stops. The wound is cleansed. Then Tarewai tells the boy to

66

collect certain leaves from the ngaio tree and others. Long ago the tohunga had instructed him how to make healing medicine. Now when the boy has brought him the leaves and gone away, he chants the words of the karakia, places the crushed leaves across the wound.'

David had a picture in his mind of Tarewai lying against a rock, his body plastered with leaves and partly covered by a cloak. His face sagged with suffering. The whorls of the tattooing were not symmetrical because his cheeks were hollow and his mouth twisted sideways.

'Tarewai has strength and courage. Within a few days he is able to move. The boy helps him travel by night to a safer hiding-place, somewhere where there is fresh water and shelter, somewhere near the sea where there are shellfish and seaweeds to be eaten.'

Old Tama hesitated and looked into David's eyes. 'You've guessed, Young Tama.' It was not even a question.

David nodded. 'I think so. Tell me.' He seemed to know what Old Tama was thinking, in the same way as Old Tama could reach David's mind.

'Well, I think they came to this very cave,' said the Maori.

David nodded. He agreed.

'Didn't he ever get his whalebone patu back?' he asked.

'The story says he did. I'll tell you how another day when you've got more time.'

'You mean he got it back and then lost it again?'

'The story says he gave it to the boy. It was a special gift to my ancestor. Not just to him but to his family. It was to be an heirloom for ever and ever.'

David understood that. 'And that's what the Oha's all about. That's what you're here for – looking for the patu.'

The old man nodded. 'My ancestor died young, we

think. Certainly before Tarewai did. By then the patu'd disappeared. Already my family knew about it and they were searching for it. When the head of the family died he spoke the Oha so now every generation is bound to carry on the search till the patu's found, and after that the patu itself must be handed down the family.'

'And what you're saying is,' said David, his mind leaping ahead, 'you think the boy hid the patu somewhere for safety and before he'd told anyone where he'd put it, he was killed perhaps – or captured by enemies.'

Old Tama was nodding, smiling and nodding.

'And,' went on David, 'you think that here in the cave, where Tarewai'd been safe, well that's where you think the boy'd most likely pick a hiding-place. But you know what I think? Perhaps it's in the first spot, up Harbour Cone?'

Again the old man nodded. 'Perhaps.'

'You know,' said David, 'all this digging and such, it's too much for you. Can't you get someone else from the family to help? A nephew or a cousin? Someone, well, a bit younger –?' He hesitated, not wishing to hurt feelings. But the old man smiled and went on nodding.

'That's always been in my mind and I've put out feelers. I expect to hear any day now. Meanwhile I carry on.'

David rushed on eagerly. 'If you like, I'll give you a hand. I could go up Harbour Cone and look around. Would you like that?'

Old Tama looked very pleased indeed. 'Now that,' he said, 'is a very kind offer. I'd be happy to accept. Thank you very much.'

'I'll see what I can do.' David's head buzzed with ideas. 'I guess I'd better go now, but I'll be making a plan.'

'Come again soon, Young Tama.'

'I will. Good-bye. I mean, ka kite ano.'

'Ae! E haere ra koe,' answered Old Tama happily. He picked up his shovel, levered himself to his feet and turned back into the cave.

Next day David was back at school. Hemi sought him out at once.

'I told them all you saved my life,' he announced. 'At home, I mean. They want you to come round so they can thank you. Mum'd like to meet your mother too.'

David inwardly gulped at the idea of his father's reaction to such a visit while the land squabble was still rankling. He said, 'Gee, Hemi, you shouldn't have told them that. It was nothing special. Did you tell them about my father kicking you out? That's what I feel mean about.'

Hemi laughed. 'I forgot to mention that bit. People don't have to tell their families everything.'

'No,' agreed David, momentarily wondering what his own father had meant when he had stormed on about hearing home truths. 'I daresay all families've got secrets.'

'My father's got one anyway,' said Hemi, who much enjoyed passing on any he knew. 'He goes off in the car very early most mornings and comes back in time for breakfast. Mother knows but he's got us kids guessing.'

'Anyway,' said David, 'I'm glad you didn't let on about the other thing.'

Hemi gave David a friendly punch on the nose.

8

It was a Saturday.

At breakfast David, full of thoughts of Harbour Cone, gathered there were plans for renewing some of the fencing in the sheepyards. In sudden panic he realized that his father was about to block the weekend by requesting him to help with this boring operation. David acted fast. He choked as he gulped his tea. He slammed his mug down, put his hands over his mouth and rushed from the room. Outside in the passage he grinned and then remembered to go on coughing and spluttering. A pity to go without bread and marmalade, but worth the sacrifice not to be captured for a whole day in the yards. He was into his room and out of the window in no time. He ran round the side of the house furthest from the kitchen and across the paddock near the edge of the cliff, then he doubled back where the slope of the paddock hid him from the homestead. In due course he worked his way to the far side of the macrocarpa shelter belt and then he was safe.

A faint call sounded from downwind. David whistled

as he hurried away from his fencing obligations. His thoughts were on what he might find in a crevice or a hollow tree.

Once David was well away from home he struck off towards the Portobello side of the peninsula. He did not wish to meet and be questioned by people he knew, so he kept out of sight of houses, sometimes creeping along with his head below the level of the dry stone wall. At last he did emerge on the Highcliff Road, almost directly above the township of Portobello, and vaulted over a gate and struck off up Harbour Cone over the short-cropped grass. A couple of cabbage trees supported tufts of tousled leaves on their long straight rope-like trunks. David climbed higher. Now stunted native bushes began to insinuate themselves from between the laval rocks. Clumps of mingi-mingi and wind-scarred totara and gnarled fuchsia trees crept across rocks that became more and more treacherous. Here was a place where a man could hide even now, let alone in the primary bush of Tarewai's day.

'Tarewai,' he whispered aloud, creeping around, peering under cavelike boulders. 'Where did you lie up?'

He flattened himself under the dry branches of a fallen tree. A few brave young shoots grew from the apparently dead wood. The leaves were shiny with tiny dots on them, ngaio leaves. David remembered. There had to be ngaio. Tarewai had crushed leaves like these to make the Maori balm for healing his wounds. He slithered down a spiked boulder and landed in a sheltered hollow beneath it.

At once he thought, 'This is the sort of spot I'd choose if I wanted to lie hidden.' The place felt right. He was sure it was right. He began to search for anywhere a weapon could be hidden. There was no gap beneath the boulder, which seemed to grow like a living thing out of the ground. There were no cracks or crevices in its sides. He began to scratch under the roots of the nearby ngaio and peered through the bush to see if there were any obvious landmarks from which someone might have taken some kind of bearing. Surely nobody would dig a hole and hide a treasure without being able to give directions to someone else by word of mouth as to where it could be found.

After about an hour David gave up. He planned to come again and bring a pick-axe or a spade. He would divide the area into squares with pegs and bits of string, like digs organized by archaeologists in the pictures he had seen at school.

Well, there was no point in going home too soon. It was a beautiful day and not to be wasted on fence posts. 'I'm for it when I get back anyway,' he thought. 'Might as well enjoy myself while I'm about it.' The idea had come to him to go to Little Papanui Beach and see the territory where the Kati Mamoe had once lived.

It was a long way. He skirted Papanui Inlet and kept above the road. Far down below on the sand flats, tiny figures were busy digging for cockles or fishing for flounders in the shallows. Further on, he crossed the road and ran downhill towards the sea, keeping to the fence lines. Seen from high up here, the sea crawled silently up and down the beach, too far away to be heard. Some of the paddocks were set aside for winter feed crops. In other the cows watched him placidly. But in a paddock above Papanui Beach a bunch of flighty heifers ganged up and followed him closely, heads lowered. In the ordinary way David would have laughed and shooed them off. Today

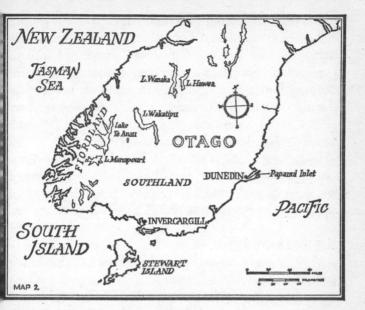

his laughter died. The heifers would not be shooed. They continued to advance. The threat seemed real. David dived under the nearest fence. He could feel hostile eyes watching as he followed the creek down to the beach.

Even on the sands the feeling of being watched persisted. Over to his right almost sheer cliffs stood sentinel above him. The very sight of the drop from the clifftops to the boulder-strewn beach made him uneasy. To the left the dunes and marram grass swept in a curve towards Victory Beach. There were ridges and hollows, places where a whole tribe of enemies could lie low, with vantage points from which they could see and not be seen.

David was the intruder, on enemy territory. A pair of

73

black oyster-catchers got up suddenly with shrill piping. A flock of terns rose at the alarm note and spread the warning of David's approach. David, aware of hundreds of unknown eyes following his every movement, turned left, away from the cliffs, and pretended to saunter casually as he followed the line of the waves, stamping on seaweed bubbles to pop them, stopping to examine the dried-up jellyfish, which looked like scraps of cellophane.

The feeling of threat persisted. David played the innocent; picked up stranded sea-tulips and squeezed them till they squirted, took out his knife and cut off a thick stalk of kelp, which he began to whittle into a ball as he ambled along.

He came to a part of the beach where there were boulders on the sand and penguin tracks in thick braids leading to and from a flattened terrace of grass, young thistle and nettle shoots. In the centre of this area sprawled a white tree trunk, hurled there from the sea by some freak tide. Suddenly, David's throat contracted. From the shadow of this driftwood leapt a nearly-naked Maori boy, clutching a stick, who shouted incomprehensible invective, contorting his features and stamping out a ritual dance of challenge. Not for long. David's astonishment was too much for the dancer, who suddenly doubled up with laughter.

'Fooled you! Ghosts, you thought!' Hemi tried to continue the challenge but ended up sitting on the log convulsed with laughter.

David laughed with angry relief. 'What's it all about?' he shouted. 'How come you're here on your own?'

Hemi waited while David picked his way through the prickles and climbed up on the tree trunk beside him.

74

'The family's getting cockles for tea,' said Hemi. 'I got bored. I pushed off.'

'Mine's fencing,' said David. 'I left before that started.'

Hemi lay back on the smooth sea-polished wood. He had taken off his cotton singlet; his brown skin made David unaccountably shy of his own whiteness. David's skin was exceptionally fair and freckled, like his mother's, though his eyes were as brown as Hemi's. He flopped down beside Hemi.

'Actually, I was thinking about the tribe that used to, live here, the Kati Mamoe.'

'Hey!' exclaimed Hemi. 'You've got that right. My Karani told us kids about this place. I remember now. Right here there used to be fishing huts. The village was along there by the creek. There's some tapu ground there too, because of burial places.'

'Does your Karani remember the Kati Mamoe village?'

'Don't be daft. How old do you think she is? It's just she knows the stories. And the museum people dug around and found remains which prove the stories are true.'

David nodded. 'Did you get a chance to ask her more about that word?' he asked.

'What word?'

'You know. About Oha, and whether the promises were always kept, and what happened if they weren't.'

'Ah gee, Oha. Yes I did. And I got the lot,' sighed Hemi. 'She goes on for hours once she's got started. You know what grandparents are.'

David did not. He had never met any of his grandparents. He knew that his father, at the age of sixteen, had emigrated alone from Ireland, so all the Regans were back there. His mother's folk had lived in Auckland and died when David was tiny. He had seen photos of them and their old home in Yorkshire.

'What did she say?' he asked.

'We were about right,' said Hemi. 'She told me all about the chief dying and the people grouped around listening to his Oha. Then the tangi starts. I was there when my grandfather died. I saw him in his coffin dressed up in his best black suit. He had a beaut funeral. We gave him a great send-off.' Hemi stood up and began pretending to intone a speech in Maori, letting his voice die away on a sing-song note at the end of each phrase. He began to remember the words, or at least the shape of the words. He raised first one hand, then the other, letting them droop and sweep to emphasize the meaning of the speech, its repetition and its cadences. What had started as a parody became performance. The funeral oration could not be ridiculed.

'What does all that mean?' asked David, when Hemi's voice faltered and stopped.

Hemi picked up his singlet. 'Oh, lots of things.'

'Like what?'

'Like, well thanking him for everything and all that. And then telling him to take the long path and listing all the mountains and rivers he'd got to cross between here and Te Reinga.'

'That's the cape beyond Ninety Mile Beach way up North,' said David. 'Mum told me. And there's a pohutukawa tree on the cliff where spirits are meant to take off into the sea.'

Hemi nodded. 'That's it. I was saying "Look up to the mountain, stand up at the door, take one more look

76

weeping for those left behind".' Sudden tears sprang to Hemi's eyes. He shouted, 'Race you up the beach,' and leapt over the rough ground and down over the rocks to the sand.

David followed. He did not try to catch his friend but ran along the line of the tide, straight as an arrow, ignoring the coming and going of the gently plashing waves. He imagined he was a Maori spirit flying northwards up Ninety Mile Beach, taking the long path towards the rock where the pohutukawa grew. As he ran he looked up to the mountains, or rather to the cliffs at the other end of the bay. They were steep and yellow with ugly horizontal slits.

Hemi was waiting for him near the creek.

'Shall we go on further?' he suggested. 'Or do you want to get back?'

David looked up at the cliffs again. The old uneasiness oppressed him. Near the beach were many small rock slips. Higher up a straggling line of samphire clung to the ochreous soil. Nothing moved. Higher up still, because of the slits, the cliffs looked as though they might crack at any time and crash down on the rocks below. A very dead sheep was rotting on a ledge near the top. David's father lost sheep over the cliffs at home. You could not fence properly near the sea. Salt spray rusted wire. Sometimes sheep just tumbled over and were killed at once. Others got themselves to the point of no return on narrow ledges and died slowly of starvation, the black-backed gulls circling hopefully, waiting for carrion.

'Creepy sort of place,' said David. 'I keep feeling we're being watched.'

'I expect we are,' said Hemi. 'Ghosts everywhere.' He

pointed to the sand dunes near the creek. 'That's where the pa was, where the Kati Mamoe lived. And the ovens. That's where they cooked "long pig" for their cannibal feasts.'

'I walked right over there,' said David. 'There's nothing to see now.'

Hemi shuddered. 'Do you know what the museum people found? The whole pa was built actually on top of the graves of the previous inhabitants. Think of that. Building on burial places. No wonder they had disasters.'

'Who did? The tribe or the museum people?'

'Well, the tribe. And I shouldn't wonder about the museum people. The place is tapu, forbidden, even if the elders did sort of give permission.'

Hemi swung round and plodded away from the site towards the boulders at the foot of the cliffs.

David followed. A pungent musky smell reached his nostrils. Hemi was wrinkling up his nose.

'Dead sheep,' he said.

This time it was David who was better informed.

'That's seal smell,' he told Hemi. 'Wait on. Let's have a good look.'

The boys scanned the boulders. Suddenly, quite close by, one boulder shifted and became alive and turned a whiskered face and a pair of protruding brown eyes towards them. Hemi was delighted. He had never seen a seal so close to.

'Keep still,' said David. 'Don't scare them. There'll be dozens more.'

The boys sat on a grey volcanic rock and scanned the beach. First one boulder, then another, proved not to be a boulder at all, but a basking seal. The texture of volcanic rock and crew-cut fur was almost identical, the camouflage nearly perfect.

'No wonder you felt you were being watched,' said Hemi. 'There's another. Look. And there.'

The seals were draped over the boulders, ardent sun worshippers. Occasionally a front flipper waved vaguely, looking like a fat strip of bull kelp, or tail flippers gave a lazy flap, refolding themselves more comfortably. The smaller seals seemed worn out after the morning's fishing expedition. Even the big bulls lay babyishly upside-down, eyes shut, occasionally twitching stiff whiskers or snuffling black dog-like noses. The fur under their chins was a soft brown. The seals looked comfortable, relaxing across razor-sharp rocks pillowed between barnacles and boulders. Hemi counted out loud. Thirty-two seals. But David's thoughts had returned to the word 'Oha'. Hemi had been side-tracked into the funeral chant. David wanted more information.

'Hemi,' he began again. 'Did your grandmother say what happened if an Oha was never carried out? That must've happened sometimes. I mean, someone might ask for something to be done that was just about impossible.'

'Thirty-three – and there's thirty-four, or have I counted that one?' Hemi was only listening to David with half an ear. 'What's just about impossible? Oh, you mean Ohas? No, Ohas aren't impossible. See that big bull one over there?'

'And why not?' persisted David.

'Fail-safe system,' said Hemi calmly.

David threw a broken crab shell at Hemi. The big bull seal opened his bulgy eyes at the miniscule sound.

'How fail-safe?' he asked impatiently.

Hemi sat down next to David.

'It's fail-safe because if the people who promise can't carry out the Oha themselves they're bound to pass on the message to the next generation. So that way an Oha never lapses.'

David still was not satisfied. He was worried for Old Tama.

'But if, say, a son died before his father and there weren't any grandchildren?'

A pebble rattled down the cliff face and bounced on a rock next to David. The big bull seal heaved himself up on to his front flippers and blew out his whiskers accusingly.

'I don't think that seal likes you,' said Hemi. David agreed.

The whole of Papanui Beach felt like alien territory. But he was so near to getting the truth out of Hemi he was not going to be thwarted by a seal.

He tried again. 'Listen, Hemi. Say an old person knew the Oha but couldn't carry it out. And his son was already dead –'

Now at last Hemi was listening properly. His eyes lit up.

'Ah! That's when the whole thing gets really interesting. Karani tells us these good stories. A person who dies without passing on the Oha can come back, just once, from the dark.'

'How do you mean, "come back"?'

'As a ghost of course,' grinned Hemi, 'a returned spirit. Like I told you.'

David snorted. 'And I told you something. I don't believe in ghosts.'

'Okay, okay,' said Hemi. 'Have it your own way. But you did ask about Ohas and that's what Karani said. And she says these spirits, you wouldn't know they weren't real people. They look completely ordinary and you'd never guess except for certain things.'

'Like what?'

'Well, they don't need sleep and they don't eat. That's because a spirit can't return if he eats a single mouthful of food in the home of the ancestors.'

A ridiculous idea crossed David's mind. He rejected it at once. 'How else can you tell?'

'Karani says there's this sort of feeling. She says, animals specially. They can sense it at once, this something special.'

David saw in his mind's eye Mabel's total submission to the thick brown finger stroking her yellow head.

'And people too,' went on Hemi. 'Actually I don't get exactly what she meant. Some sort of influence or power over them.'

'How are these – well, spirits meant to get back to this world after all that chanting and ceremony sending them off?' asked David gruffly.

'I'll tell you,' said Hemi, looking up at David from under his black forelock. 'Maybe one day you could want to use the info. My Karani swears she'll come back and have a bit of us herself if we haven't done what she's said and behaved ourselves.'

David found himself quoting Old Tama's words.

'You mean you've got to set your mind to it before you take the long path?'

'Too right,' agreed Hemi. 'There's one particular thing you've got to remember. When you've flown north, over

the rivers and mountains, you've got to tie a knot in the grass at Te Reinga and throw it into the wind. All along Ninety Mile Beach, Karani says, she's seen knotted grass bowling along the sand.'

David demurred. 'That's probably special grass that scatters seed in the wind. There wouldn't be that number of guys wanting to come back.'

'Maybe not,' said Hemi darkly, 'but who knows when they're hard to spot from ordinary people? It's not till they finish whatever they come back for and quietly disappear again – well, that's when you tumble to what's been under your very nose.'

'Do you really believe in ghosts, Hemi?'

Hemi shrugged his shoulders. 'Half 'n half,' he answered truthfully. 'More at night-time than in the day.'

The big bull seal reared up, staring up at the cliff. He opened his mouth, showing enormous yellow teeth. A regular cascade of small stones was slipping down. David stared too. Was it the height of the cliffs, or the moving clouds, or the stones pouring towards him? He had a premonition of falling and falling.

The seal turned ostentatiously and began humping his great weight over the rocks towards the sea. Immediately every other seal on the shore was on the alert.

'They're leaving,' cried Hemi.

The whole company of seals was on the move, heaving towards the safety of the water. Hemi began to laugh.

'Look at them, Dave! Like a sack race, or like everyone in sleeping bags. Just watch that.'

But David was still staring at the cliff and the racing clouds. He was dizzy with the feeling of falling. Hemi grabbed him by the arm.

'Hey! Wake up, Dave. You all right?'

David blinked and turned. The seals were all in the sea, diving under the rollers, shining like black seaweed, rippling through the green water.

'I'm all right,' he said.

'You look like you've seen a ghost.'

David licked his salty lips. 'Maybe I have,' he agreed.

Later, as he and Hemi began the climb to go home, David had another premonition. This time it was of running and being chased. Breathlessly he mounted the hill. He could not get away from Papanui Beach fast enough.

Hemi and David parted above Papanui Inlet, and David

went on home alone. Eventually he wound his way down to the shore again and walked along the sands from bay to bay, sometimes climbing over the saddle of a headland if the rocks below were pounded too heavily by the surf. The wind had got up and was sweeping across the sand in gusts, leaving fan-shaped patterns. It skimmed off the tops of the waves as they charged the shoreline. The ranks of breakers advanced in a pincer movement, clashing as they met, scouring the sandy bottom and changing in colour from green to ochreous yellow. The spray flew. Terns rose as white as snowflakes against the bright sky. Wind and water were not alive as the terns were alive; but you only had to look at them to see they were not dead either. So what about Old Tama? David began to run away from his thoughts, jumping the bundles of cast-up kelp that sprawled like thick-limbed octopuses, ignoring the sting of grit against his legs.

9

When eventually David reached home there were recriminations and complaints. Where had he been? How could he be so selfish? Why did he shirk lending a hand? He scarcely heard any of it. Now he could not banish from his mind Old Tama's quiet voice, refusing food, talking about having to set one's mind to return from the home of the ancestors and his family business.

'Tomorrow,' said David, to stop the nagging. 'I'll work all tomorrow.' He was remembering all sorts of, well, unusual details about his friend Old Tama.

David crept off to bed early and lay on his back trying to sort out the evidence. One side of him said 'nonsense', and the other whispered 'but – but –'. David nibbled a snag on his fingernail. One part of him scoffed, while the other raced through his imagination conjuring up – alternatives. David sucked in his cheeks and swallowed loudly.

'You'll simply go there and ask him straight out,' said his sensible side. 'You've got to know for certain. Now that's settled, you can get to sleep.'

But his other side kept him awake nearly all night imagining and dreading the confrontation.

After a few hours of uneasy sleep he awoke, determined to stick to his decision. Old Tama was always up at dawn – David gulped as he remembered Hemi declaring that ghosts did not need to sleep. There was to be work fencing all day, so now was the only moment, except after work in the dusk. 'No time like the present,' he found himself muttering hastily, as though it were the penguins needing his advice. He got up, dressed, and climbed through his window.

It was then that his feet developed a will of their own. 'Straight down through Penguin Pass,' David decided. But his feet dawdled and took him round by the woolshed. The dogs pounced to their feet. David was almost sorry they obeyed his instinctive signal to quieten them. His feet led him away from the yard and up the road. David rationalized the route he was taking. 'Better to take the track from the road when I'm out of sight of the house,' he told himself. 'I don't want them seeing me go down to Penguin Pass too often. They might investigate.' He plodded uphill, feeling very conspicuous in the early morning sunlight. Another lovely day. But of course his father would be groaning for rain. 'Actually, Dad might be up by now,' thought David. 'I'll have to go back if he shouts.'

A harrier rose from the side of the road and wheeled round on untidy wings. David's thoughts circled too, round and round with no conclusions.

As he breasted the second rise of the hill, where the creek darkened the dry dust of the road, David almost walked into a car pulled up on the grass verge. He recognized the Waka car and, with a leap of relief, he saw Henare himself standing at the open boot. David's thoughts sang, 'It's all off, I can't go.' The reprieve was so unexpected that he gave Henare a huge grin of welcome. Henare looked up startled, then slammed the boot shut and smiled warmly as he leant across it to greet David.

'Gooday, David. Just the person I hoped to see. How'd you be?'

'Good, thanks, Mr Waka. Lovely day.'

'The best. My lucky day meeting you. My wife's been on at me to look you up. We're very grateful, David. We owe you a big vote of thanks.'

David bent down and flicked a stone out from under his instep. Shyness crept up on him. He did not speak.

'Hemi told us how you saved him. We hope we'll do something for you some day. We're working on an idea.'

'It wasn't anything. Hemi's probably told you all wrong.'

'I think not,' said Henare. 'Anyway the Waka family's grateful. My wife'd like to get to know your mother. Will you tell her? Well, I'd best be off now or I'll be late. Be seeing you.' He climbed into his car.

'So long.' David raised a hand.

Henare had to reverse several times to turn the car in the narrow road. David waved as he drove off, leaving a drifting tail of dust.

David sat down on the bank at the side of the road. He could not go down the track to the cottage just yet because the road twisted and Henare and the car would be in and out of sight for a while.

'Well, what was that all about?' he wondered, idly watching the creek escape from the drain which was meant to carry it under the road, but did no such thing. 'He didn't come all this way on the chance of meeting me to say thank-you.' And he began to reflect on why he himself was up so early.

The clear realities of morning sunlight and bird song, the brisk walk up the road, the chat with Henare, made queries about ghosts suddenly seem very far-fetched and foolish.

David wondered how a few coincidences could have led him to harbour such ridiculous suspicions. The more he thought about Old Tama, the more human and down-to-earth the old man seemed to be. Only one query flickered in David's mind. Old Tama's refusing snacks and admitting to a small appetite was fair enough. But a man must eat. How did the old man get his stores to such a deserted spot? He looked far too old to walk all the way to the shop near the school and if he had, Hemi would certainly have noticed him. Anyway the local Maori community would never let an old man go off on his own without keeping in touch with him.

Suddenly David solved the problem. Of course it was Henare who was keeping an eye on him, bringing him boxes of stores by car. Hemi knew his father had a secret which involved going out early several times a week. And Old Tama had mentioned about always being up at dawn.

David jumped up. Thank goodness he had not gone down to Old Tama burbling about 'ghosts'. What an idiot he would have felt when the old man explained about Henare. Yes, and of course neither Old Tama nor Henare wanted David's father to know a Maori was staying in the cottage on disputed land and digging on Bob's property. No wonder it was all a secret.

David began to run home down the road. To think

that for nearly twenty-four hours he had almost believed in ghosts. He would never let on to Hemi about *that*.

It was not, however, a happy day. David spent it holding posts and passing tools and being reproached for lack of concentration. Bob had good reason to complain. David was thinking very hard but not at all about fencing. He was planning another expedition to Harbour Cone and a more scientific search there.

After the evening meal Bob went out to look round the lambs. The dry weather was not helping them fatten. Joy was standing by the back door, dithering.

'Have you looked in the tanks today, David?' she asked. 'Is there enough water to spare some for the veg patch?'

David was flopped in a chair, fed up after a wasted day. It would take too long to get to Harbour Cone after school. Next weekend would be his soonest chance. 'What's that? Water? Oh I dunno, Mum.'

She turned round. 'What's up with you?' she demanded suspiciously.

David was trying to think up a convincing answer when he suddenly remembered the message Henare had given him that morning.

'By the way, Mum, Henare Waka said his wife'd like to have you over.'

'He did?' Joy tried to cheer David up by laughing. 'That's a great idea. I can imagine it, Dad saying "Where's my tea?" and me saying "Shan't be a minute, I've been practising my pois over at the Wakas' place".' She twirled a thin wrist and swayed her hips and succeeded in capturing David's interest.

'Mum, can you do the pois?'

She glanced up the hillside where Bob was waving his arms at the dogs. 'I used to. I don't know if I could now.'

'How'd you learn?'

'Oh, in Auckland.' She hesitated. 'When I was a kid. A Maori taught my friend.'

Once David had heard his mother buying a nit comb at the pharmacy. 'My friend,' she had said, 'my friend asked me to get one for her kiddies.'

So he guessed by her voice that this was only half true. Aloud he said, 'Go on, Mum. Give us a demo. You still got your pois?'

Joy shook her head. 'Course not. But tell you what, I could make one just roughly. I haven't thought of pois for I don't know how many years. It was fun.'

She scuttled off and came back with a roll of toilet paper. 'Get some string, Dave, and a small plastic bag. I'll show you.'

Joy quickly scrumpled up paper until she had a ball about the size of an orange. Then she put it into the bag and tied it up securely, leaving a tail of string. She swung the ball like a long pendulum. David could not remember seeing her face looking so engrossed and vital. Not since – when? He thought he could remember her smiling like that once and saying, 'Oh, Tammy, clever Tammy.'

'This isn't really heavy enough,' she chatted. 'It'll do, though. The Maoris use flax. That gives the right sound. Your wrists have to be very supple for the short pois. I expect I've stiffened up. I'll try a long poi first.'

She flicked off her shoes and spread her knobbly toes as if the rhythm would flow upwards into her body from the ground. She began to swing the ball, slipping one hand from the centre of the string to the end and slapping the poi with first one palm, then the other. It was a complicated manoeuvre but obviously, once learned, soon recalled. David cheered her on. She laughed. David clapped his hands with the rhythm of the slapping. She began to hum:

'Po kare kare ana,
Nga wai o Rotorua –'

David watched her thin arms and red hands in astonishment. Now her hips were swinging. Even her feet were supple. She tossed back her pale hair and held her chin high, not even watching the poi. Then excitedly she wound up the string till it was only about four inches long and quickened the rhythm. Now her wrist twisted and turned with amazing speed and accuracy. The ball slapped the back of that wrist, then was hit with her other hand. It whirled so fast that David, watching closely, could not discern the exact pattern of its flight.

'E hine e,' sang Joy,
'Hoki mai ra –'

For the first time that David could remember her name truly seemed to fit her personality.

'Ka mate ahau i, Te aroha e.'

At the end of the song they both laughed and David applauded.

'Let's have a go!'

Bob spoke from the door. 'So what's this? A concert party?'

The sarcasm in his voice killed their laughter. Joy dropped her arms, trying to free her fingers from the string, scuffled back into her shoes.

'Just a bit of fun, Bob.'

'I need David's help.'

'Oh, Dad,' protested David. Caught off his guard, he did not notice the command behind the statement. 'I been helping you all day. I bet when you were my age you liked a bit of fun too.'

'Not much fun going then.' Bob spoke bitterly. 'Ireland in those days wasn't child's play. We knew what work was. *We* had guts.'

The implications stung David. He grew reckless. 'I'm not your slave.'

Bob's anger surfaced. 'You owe me something. You can't get it all your own way. Singing and dancing now, but you've been messing around all day doing damn all. Proper little runt you are.'

Half-formed opinions about fairness and parents forcing children to work jostled unexpressed in David's mind. All he could do was hang his head and mutter:

'Well, I didn't ask to be born.'

Suddenly Joy plunged into the conversation and took sides. 'Your father's done more than you know,' she said. 'He's right, so hush, David, or you'll say things you'll be sorry for one day.'

This was the last straw. Grown-ups chopped and changed. David ran out of the kitchen to his own room slamming doors. He sat glowering on his bed.

Usually his mother defended him when Bob started on about his son not being as tall and tough as he himself had been at the same age. Now suddenly even Joy had switched against him. David seethed with fury at the injustice of it. He couldn't help his size. No one appreciated him or understood him – Then he remembered Old Tama.

David struggled into a jersey, grabbed a blanket from

his bed and ducked out through the window. Dusk was deepening as he scrambled over the fence. Back at the house the lamp was lit. The kitchen window was a rosy rectangle. David turned angrily away from it and ran down the paddock and into the shadows of Penguin Pass. On the far side of the lupin he stood still. He found himself listening to the noise of silence, resting his eyes on the calm of the night sky. Beyond the horizon a pale yellow streak divided the sea dark from the sky dark. Familiar stars appeared wherever David was not looking: the Southern Cross with its pointers: Orion with his raised sword. Hardly any wind breathed in the leaves; the sea hissed as if to quieten the mumbling of the breakers. He identified the rustlings and scufflings of night creatures going about their business. Far away a lamb woke and called for its mother. Several ewes answered from across the valley. Close by there were soft squeaks from Goopy's chicks and a sudden crescendo of crooning ecstasy as they were fed. The sound died away. David could distinguish the stutter of a bill opening and shutting as a penguin preened. Further away other penguins shuffled carefully up or slithered clumsily down the tracks to the sea.

Suddenly an adult penguin called, an eerie stammering cry that reminded David of the morning of Abel's death. He turned away from the memory and began to scramble up the side of the creek.

Under cover of night even the bush now seemed to turn against him. Branches whipped across his face and bush lawyer hooked in the blanket he carried slung across one shoulder. The fast-growing nettles and thistles were massed to attack. Something pale loomed up ahead. David hesitated. What the heck was that? Then he realized it was not a large shape in the distance but something quite small very close – the white breast of a penguin. The whiteness hovered, irresolute, made little dashes of indecision, this way, that way and finally hurtled past him. Mabel, off to the fish supply. He turned to watch her but the moment her breast was out of sight she melted into the darkness, her uneven footsteps padding towards the sea.

Then it occurred to David that at this time of night Old Tama would more likely be at the cottage than at the cave. Or did he literally keep watch over the chick while Mabel was at sea? 'Anyone there?' yelled David, an edge of anxiety hardening his voice.

The familiar voice answered from close by.

'Young Tama? I'm here. What's wrong?'

David stumbled uphill, pushing through the silent barrier into the welcoming aroma of live penguin and the comfortable presence of Old Tama.

'Mind the chick,' said the old man.

David clasped the blanket to his chest and sat down breathing heavily. Somehow his feelings had all piled up inside him; he felt choked, on the brink of tears. He could not see Old Tama at the back of the cave and was glad that he himself was only a shadow in the dark.

'Young Tama,' said the Maori voice, 'what's the problem? Can you tell me? Perhaps I could help.'

David tried to phrase his reply. The tightness in his throat relaxed as he searched for words.

Well, he could name one of his problems.

'Dad.' His voice was bitter. 'It's Dad's my problem.'

There was a long silence. Then Old Tama asked:

'What's happened?'

'It's *always* happening,' cried David. 'He walks all over me. He never lets up. He's always saying I've got no guts and –'

'And why is now, tonight, worse than always?'

'Well, tonight, Mum –' David hesitated. He did not want to say anything unkind about his mother. He sighed:

'I don't know whose side she's on. She dithers.'

David had expected sympathy. He did not get it. Old Tama said:

'You've seen penguin chicks trodden on by their parents?'

'Yes, but –'

'For their own good?'

'In a way, but –'

'They survive. So will you. Unless what he says is true. And as for dithering –' Old Tama's voice changed. Now he was smiling. 'Mabel dithers too. But I think we both agree that in her own way she copes. An excellent parent.'

David had to smile too. Poor Mabel. Poor Mum.

'I thought you'd be on my side,' he protested.

'I'm on the side of truth. If you're in trouble, it's because you don't understand the truth yet. If you knew it – *when* you know it – then you'll be right. That's what I think.'

'Old Tama, there's a mystery somewhere. Dad drops hints. Mum tells me half-truths. What are they hiding? Why don't they tell me? How can I be expected to understand if no one tells me?'

'And what've you done about it? Most parents wait till children are ready to ask questions. Have you asked?'

David shut up. The answer was 'No'. He never asked his parents questions.

The conversation with Old Tama seemed to continue inside his head. So what did he do when things upset him, puzzled him? He retreated into silence. Why silence? Because – David found himself trembling – because nothing provoked his father so effectively. That was the truth of the matter. And nothing forced his mother to speak up so hotly in his defence. And nothing, no, nothing, David realized bleakly, caused so much friction between his father and his mother as his own silences. And how could all this wrong be put right?

'Perhaps,' came Old Tama's gentle voice, 'it's time you asked your parents a few questions?'

David nodded in the darkness, greatly comforted. Already he knew more of the truth. Already things were a little better. Old Tama and he were both on the side of truth.

Quietly he arranged his blanket and lay down somewhere between the nest and Old Tama's voice. His cheeks dried as he stared at the stars.

After a while he said, 'Please go on with the story. How did Tarewai find his patu and give it to your ancestor?'

'Young Tama, you'd best go home. Your mother'll be anxious.'

'She won't notice I'm not there till morning. I love sleeping out. Please let me stay.'

'You promise to go home at daybreak when I wake you?'

'I promise,' said David. 'Now tell me the story.'

'Very well, very well. It's not easy to tell, you know.' He sighed. 'There are different accounts. Variations.'

'Tell me your family one. Wasn't the boy there, your ancestor?'

'Yes, he was there. But he never told anyone anything.' Old Tama sighed again even more heavily. 'Shut your eyes, Young Tama. You've got to let your imagination travel back down the years. The mists of time have risen.'

David closed his eyes, surrendering willingly to the power of Old Tama's quiet voice.

10

'There's mist rolling in from the sea that evening when Tarewai and the boy set forth. News has reached them that the Kati Mamoe are expecting visitors at the pa on Papanui Beach. Tarewai has been planning for such an occasion for many months. Now the time has come. The evening draws in earlier than usual because of the sea mist. From the hills above the pa he and the boy hear singing. Stealthily, silently they descend. Now the fires of the pa can be seen through the bush.'

David squeezed his eyes tighter shut and saw sparks and flashes behind his eyelids. Like firelight, like torches. Old Tama's voice droned on.

'Tarewai makes a sign and halts. A Kati Mamoe look-out is not far ahead. You can hear him humming. Now listen. Tarewai springs, and you hear a chop and a gurgle. The boy avoids the dark bundle in the fern. A dead man is tapu.'

All round David the rustlings and the whisperings of the bush at night time seemed to obey Old Tama's voice. Soft footsteps he could discern, and the brushing of leaves, the whisper of tussock, the scratch of flax in the wind as two shadowy figures creep down towards the beach. And in the distance, murmurings, voices, a dog barking.

'The moon has disappeared in the sea mist and now there is sand underfoot and a belt of flax lies ahead. Tarewai disappears like a snake down the passage cleared by penguins and Kati Mamoe flax-cutters. The boy follows. Tarewai untwists his hair and lets it fall forwards, concealing his tattooing.'

'No need for the boy to be disguised,' thought David, 'no one would recognize a boy,' and he felt safer. The voice in his ear was Tarewai's. 'Keep back from the fires, Tama. Stay behind me but follow closely.'

The next moment Tarewai and the boy were on the sandy beach. Tarewai was ambling along, chatting to Tama over his shoulder, teasing him in a rough voice, quite unlike his own. Now they were mingling with the Kati Mamoe and their guests, edging towards a group of men who were listening to some story told by a loud-mouthed warrior. He was boasting of his own strength and cunning. Some of the others were not taking him seriously.

'But you let him slip away,' shouted one, 'you never found the body.'

'He was as good as dead, I say,' cried the boaster. 'I had his innards out on the beach. No man could've survived that.'

'Where is he then?' teased another voice.

'The sea's got him,' suggested someone else, 'picking his bones and fattening the fishes for our hooks.'

'I've got proof, I can prove what I say,' shouted the warrior. 'The others'll bear me out, but it was I who kept the trophy.' He began to fumble at his waist. Tarewai's hand on Tama's shoulder gripped like a vice.

'You've got his patu?' exclaimed a man, admiringly. 'That was good. Slicing him open with his own patu.' He chuckled, remembering the often-told story.

'The very same,' said the boastful one. 'Here it is. And the great man's blood soaked into the bone.'

'Bone? Whalebone?'

'You'd think a man of his standing'd have a greenstone mere.'

'Maybe he had. But this was his weapon on that day.'

'Let's have a look. Yes, whalebone. Nicely balanced anyway.' The man swung the patu gently round his head but other hands stretched up to test it out.

'Pass it along – The cutting edge, that's quite something – Must've taken years to get it like that. My turn, pass it on – So that's the famous Tarewai patu – Pity you didn't get a famous meal too!'

Tarewai had edged forwards, infiltrating among the men. Tama held back, partly because he knew that a boy of his age should not push in among the warriors. He glanced over his shoulder, checking on the quickest darkest route up the creek towards the southern headland. Now Tarewai was next in line to examine the trophy. He held out his hand and the man next to him passed him the patu. For a moment it lay in Tarewai's palm. Tama could imagine the indrawn breath of achievement.

He tensed himself for action. He expected Tarewai would slip the patu secretly into his hands. But Tarewai gripped the patu and raised it above his head. He seemed to have forgotten everything else in this moment of ecstasy. His shout came like a thunderbolt.

'I am Tarewai!' he roared, and whirling from side to side he cracked open a couple of skulls, then dashed back into the darkness as his victims staggered and tripped and others stood dumb with astonishment.

Not till then did he put the patu swiftly into Tama's hands and run north along the dunes in the direction from which he had come. The plan had been for Tarewai, by his ostentatious behaviour, to draw the Kati Mamoe off in that direction while the inconspicuous Tama gently climbed the hillside from the creek to the southern headland. Tarewai, fresh and fit, would outrun the whole pack of over-eaten, fire-dazzled Kati Mamoe. No one would notice Tama with the patu slip away in the opposite direction up the hill.

One or two Kati Mamoe were now stumbling after Tarewai shouting. A crowd gathered round the disturbance demanding to know what had happened so loudly that the answering voices could not be heard. Tama stepped back deeper into the shadows, disquieted because he had lost those precious seconds of secrecy before Tarewai had proclaimed himself. No one seemed to have noticed him, but he could not be sure. Now people were pointing in the direction Tarewai had taken; his name was repeated over and over; several men were running after him, others were fetching weapons, someone was shouting orders. Suddenly the women raised a great wail of fury and vengeance, urging their menfolk into action.

Tama was now slinking up the south bank of the creek near the rubbish pit; on the opposite bank were huts and children. He glanced down at the patu. He was holding it by the hand grip which looked pale in the darkness. The other end was dark with blood from those split skulls. His attention was on the patu. He did not notice another shadow in the shadows. Not all the Kati Mamoe had been watching Tarewai. One shadow held a stone in its hand, gathered itself to spring. Tama bent to wipe the blood from the patu on some tussock. Precisely as he did so, he heard a swish and something sliced just over his head: the next instant a foot caught him in the side and a man tripped over him and landed with a crack on the rocky ground beside the rubbish pit.

No time for slinking now. Tama thrust the patu into his waistband and fled. The man's noisy fall had been noticed by a group of children on the hut side of the creek. Tama heard their shrill cries as he dashed up the valley and then, keeping low, veered back sharp left and then began to climb straight uphill towards the headland.

In the plan it had been Tarewai who had had to escape pursuit while Tama was merely an accomplice, delegated to carry the patu uphill and out of harm's way. But now they were after him. He realized that the thumping in his head was not just his heartbeat throbbing in his ears, but the thud of following footsteps.

He was climbing with hands as well as feet. The patu in his waistband stuck uncomfortably into his sore ribs as he scrambled upwards, doubled up like a possum humping its way across open ground. His left hand suddenly clutched at emptiness and he fell forwards on his chin. The edge of the cliff. No time to worry about near misses, he kept further to the right. He could hear heavy breathing not far behind, someone gasping and struggling after him. Tama's legs found new strength. He thrust himself up with his thigh muscles, settled his breathing into a rhythm. He must reach the top and the safety of the bush. Once in the bush he was certain he could evade his pursuers.

Someone grunted close behind him. For an instant fingers grabbed his heel, but he kicked out and wriggled free. He was nearly at the top. His heel was gripped a second time and held fast. Tama fell, rolled downhill on top of his captor. He managed to get Tarewai's patu into his hand. He slashed out with it. Missed. Then sudden agony and he heard his own leg snap. Another swinging shadow and this time Tama's head thudded back on the ground, stars spun round, Tama circled with them. A surge of Kati Mamoe warriors swept over him like a wave breaking. Tama felt himself rise from the ground on the crest of the wave. Then like driftwood he was hurled over the cliff. He threw out his hands to save himself, to fly. And now, like a bird, he was plunging towards the sea.

Tama cried out to the generations that were yet to come. The air tumbled with stars.

The cry seemed to hover in the air as David jerked to his senses. He was lying with his eyes closed, his arms outstretched. An enormous feeling of peace enfolded him. He had been terrified, but now he had crossed a boundary. Rather like going through Penguin Pass, he had reached another kingdom. David wondered if he were dead now, like the boy Tama who had been killed at Papanui. 'I must tie a knot in the grass,' he thought.

A strong familiar odour cleared David's mind. He opened his eyes. To his left he saw moonlight falling on Mabel's chick in its dirty nest; to his right, moonlight touching with silver the dark silhouette of Old Tama. The Maori sat very still but David could see his eyes were open.

'Old Tama,' whispered David. 'Can I ask you a question?'

'Anything you like.'

'What happens when you're dead?'

'You have everything you need.'

'When I die, will I find you again?'

'If you need me.'

'Are you afraid to die?'

'Of course not. I believe my son needs me. Dying's like being born. A family affair.'

'Thank you, Old Tama. I'll remember.'

David shut his eyes again. Detail by detail he recalled the story of Tama. Every event was clear in his mind. He felt very near to remembering exactly what had happened to the whalebone patu as he drifted back to sleep.

When Old Tama woke David it was barely light. Old Tama had his finger to his lips. 'Listen.'

The next moment from a distance came the repeated sound of a name being called. David recognized his mother's voice but not the words.

'That's Mum. What's she saying?'

'She's calling "Rawiri",' said the old man. 'She's looking for you.'

'Rawiri?' David frowned. 'What's Rawiri?'

Old Tama said, 'Rawiri's the Maori word for David.'

'For *David*?' repeated David, astounded. '*I'm* Rawiri? My initial is *R*?'

'What's it matter? David, Rawiri, Young Tama. It's still you she wants. Go and meet her or she'll come here.'

David jumped up and slithered quickly down to the stepping-stones and then round behind Lemon's nest to emerge on the sands. His mother stood waist-high in the lupin of Penguin Pass. She saw him at once and tried to force her way through the tangle of yellow flowers.

'Wait,' cried David, 'I'm coming.' He dived into his tunnel and soon emerged quite close to her.

'Haere mai. Haere mai,' he greeted her. 'Rawiri welcomes you. Haere mai.'

David led Joy out of the lupin to sit on the dunes. There were tears on her cheeks and David felt truly sorry that he had given her such a scare. She must have been up very early looking for him, hunting round the pools and along the high tide mark, among the flotsam and jetsam.

'It's all right, Mum.'

She nodded. She was very upset.

'Is Dad furious?'

She moved her head. 'He doesn't know. He thinks you put yourself to bed.'

'Gee, Mum, I'm really sorry. I reckoned to be home before you noticed.'

David noticed how fear had made Joy uglier than usual. Her face was blotchy. The wind had made a sandy fuzz of her hair. Her legs, always very white with blue veins showing, were now zigzagged with scratches. She wore an old skirt and cardigan over her nightgown.

'Oh, David,' she gasped. 'Rawiri! Oh Rawiri.'

David stared out to sea. And asked his first question. 'So the mug's right?' he said. 'R's for Rawiri?'

She nodded 'yes'.

There was a long silence. Rawiri. How had Bob ever agreed to a Maori name?

Perhaps to forestall this question, Joy lifted an arm and pointed to the line of breaking waves which today boomed like a cannon. 'Look!' she exclaimed.

A penguin was coming ashore. It seemed impossible that the small dark blob would not be crushed by the weight of the pounding surf. As the waves retreated there was a flurry of feet and flippers, and a hobgoblin appeared on its feet and waddled hastily up the beach.

'I think that's Mabel,' said David, trying to help his mother change the subject.

'Mabel?' Joy was recovering and welcomed something quite different to talk about. 'Don't tell me you know them all by name?'

David began to explain. Sharing some of his secrets with her was a kind of penance and it shelved thinking about his problems. He told her about Abel's death. 'Mabel was terribly cut up. You never heard such a shrieking as she made. Gee, Mum, it was like, well, like nothing on earth. Ever since then I've wished and wished I'd run down to her. I just might have been able to help.'

'Probably not. But I know how you feel. Whenever you think of it you feel like groaning out aloud.'

'That's it exactly.' David was surprised his mother understood so well. 'If ever I hear a penguin scream like that again I'll be there double quick.'

'I'll remember too,' said Joy. 'I'll go for you if you're not around. That's a promise. Tell me more about Mabel.'

David described Mabel's efforts to raise the chick on her own.

'Do you reckon she'll make it?' asked Joy.

'I guess so. She's changed. I used to get really cross with her. She was just plain silly and scatter-brained. But she's grown up now. She's a splendid mother. She takes good care of that chick. Mind you, she looks pretty haggard herself. I can see it's always tough for a solo mum.'

He turned to look at his mother. She avoided his eyes. Now it was Joy who asked the questions. 'Do you think Mabel ought to find another — another husband?'

'Well, she can't now. Not in the middle of the season. In the winter perhaps. I hope she does. She deserves the best, I reckon.'

'It might suit *her*,' said Joy. 'Would it suit the chick? Would the chick take to a new father?'

'Mabel's got her rights. She's got a future. So what if it didn't suit the chick? Probably do it good to have a father. Actually it doesn't happen like that with penguins.'

'Why doesn't it?'

'Well, by next season the chick'll be grown up. Teen-age anyway and looking for a girl friend. Penguins mate for life, but the kids push off – they have to. So Mabel'd be right to think of herself first.'

'No divided loyalties?'

'No.'

'And no stepfather problems for her chick?'

'No.'

'Lucky Mabel,' cried Joy with sudden passion.

David turned towards his mother. This time she did not avoid his eyes. She looked straight at him, a long level honest look. In the end it was David who lowered his eyes and turned away.

'And that's how it is with our family, is it, Mum?'

'That's how it is.'

Well, no more scenes. He stood up. 'Say you go back and get breakfast for Dad –' he hesitated, 'for Bob. I'll follow and slip in through my window.'

'David! Oh, David!'

'Not to worry, Mum. I promise. It's okay.'

All through breakfast Bob grumbled over the weather forecast which for the last two days had been for a sou'westerly change and rain, and which was certain to be wrong yet again. He growled on about the drought, the shortage of feed, the problem of getting the first lambs off to the freezing works. Joy burnt the toast and dropped an egg on the floor. David was silent, fingering his mug and thinking, 'Who called me Rawiri and gave me a mug with "R" on it?' That was the next question. Only he must choose his moment. Not now, in the haste of breakfast. Without a word he departed for school.

The day seemed one endless disaster. Everything went wrong.

Towards the end of the afternoon Hemi remembered he had a message for David.

'Dad's going over to your place this arfo. He said he'd pick you up if you're along the road somewhere.'

It was only as he set off home, planning to go by the paddocks, that David realized Hemi had every intention of coming with him. There he was, trotting alongside, swinging his sandals, which his mother made him wear at school but which he usually took off as soon as he was free.

'Don't you think you'd best go home?' asked David hopefully. Today seemed a poor choice for a Maori invasion of the farm, and he himself did not feel like company.

'Don't worry, old son,' said Hemi cheerfully. 'Everything's going to be fine. This is a good secret. You just wait.'

At that moment Henare Waka drew up his car and they both climbed in, so there was nothing David could do. He retired into his private worry and did not speak at all.

Bob Regan came out of the house as the Waka car drew up. He seemed far from pleased to see Henare and Hemi and gave David a see-me-later look. Henare, however, was beaming from ear to ear.

'Gooday, Bob. I've got good news.'

Joy hovered by the back door, wondering whether to invite the visitors indoors. Henare beckoned to her.

'This is something of an official visit,' he said when she stood beside her husband, fumbling with her apron. 'It's about your David saving our Hemi from drowning. We've discussed it on the marae. Everyone agrees.' He paused and looked from face to face enjoying the effect that he was creating.

'I'm to tell you that "a previous decision has been reversed". We can't actually give you that far paddock, Bob. It's Maori land. But you have our permission to use it rent-free and welcome as a thank-you to David.'

Hemi hopped up and down crying, 'There you are. Told you it was a good secret!'

Bob's face spread into a smile which smoothed his furrowed forehead and stretched his thin lips.

Joy was nearly in tears again.

'I know,' shouted Hemi to David, 'let's go there, to the far paddock. Give you a race.'

David held back. To his relief, Henare swung round and thundered, 'Hemi, hold on.'

The boy stopped and turned round. Henare went up to him and David heard him say, 'It's not safe. Keep away till I say. Okay?'

David felt limp with gratitude, but Hemi was puzzled.

'Okay, Dad, but I don't get it.'

'I'll explain later,' said his father. 'Choose somewhere else for now.' He went back to Bob and Joy who shepherded him into the house.

David and Hemi hung around outside. Eventually Hemi suggested climbing the big macrocarpa. David said, 'If you like.'

Hemi was exasperated. 'What's the matter with everyone? Aren't you glad about the land?'

'Yeah, I'm glad. Course I am. Very glad.'

'Well you don't behave glad.'

'I am too.' David tried to sound more grateful. 'We're short of feed and water, and there's a creek goes down the side of that paddock. Dad'll be really pleased.'

Even as he said the word 'Dad', he wondered how he could ever use it again for Bob. Dad was someone else.

Slowly he climbed the macrocarpa behind Hemi and thence on to the roof of the woolshed. In the sun the corrugated iron was too hot to sit on. They straddled the ridge pole where it was shaded by the trees. Hemi was puzzling over his own problem.

'Why can't we go to the far paddock? What's not safe about it? Have you been there?'

David nodded. 'It's where that deserted cottage is, the one you said was creepy.'

'Maybe he thinks the ghosts'd scare us,' said Hemi, half seriously.

'Could be.' That would do for a reason. 'Like you said, a knot in the grass and a spirit back to tell about an Oha.' He swung his legs sideways along the ridge pole and turned to stare at the sea.

Hemi shrugged. 'Oh well, I guess Dad'll explain. *You'd* be all right in that case, though. *You* wouldn't hear about an Oha.'

'Why?' asked David.

'I told you,' said Hemi. 'An Oha's family business. It's private and strictly within a family. Nobody'd hear about the details of an Oha, not unless he was a direct descendant.'

'*What?*' cried David, losing his balance and starting to slither down the roof. Hemi ran to grab him by the arm, his bare feet holding firm on the slippery iron.

'Hold up,' he cried.

David scrambled up to the ridge with Hemi's help.

Henare appeared through the kitchen door with Bob and Joy. The boys were called down and given biscuits and lemon drink. David ran his thumb round and round the 'R' on his mug. Rawiri. A Maori name.

But of course he had a Maori name! Because if an Oha

was private within a family, if an Oha was only revealed to descendants – Then Old Tama would never have told David about it unless –

David leapt towards the truth which he suddenly realized he must have known for a long time. Old Tama's son had gone to Auckland and died. But not before he had had a child, a baby son nicknamed Tammy whose pakeha mother had thought it best to marry again. Old Tama was David's very own grandfather.

The grown-ups were laughing, saying David was very solemn for someone who had just received an award for bravery and other jokes to which David could not be bothered to listen. At last he found himself automatically waving good-bye as Henare and Hemi drove off. Then Bob turned to him and put his hand on his shoulder.

'Well, David,' he said. 'Maybe I don't give you enough credit. You certainly had guts on that occasion.'

David did not answer. He wondered if the penguin chicks ever got any crumbs of praise from their parents.

Bob went on. 'Maybe I've been tough on the Maoris too –'

With sudden enlightenment David understood another truth. Bob was jealous of his wife's first husband.

'– in the past I've not been friendly. They'd every right to take offence. But they've been generous and I'm grateful. Henry's a good bloke. Hemi can come over whenever he likes.'

That was a bit better. David knew the moment had come to take Old Tama's advice and ask questions. Yet he hesitated, trying to find the words.

But Bob was waiting impatiently for thanks. A man did not climb down and practically apologize without some positive results. Joy could see her husband's irritation rising.

'Bob,' she said quickly, 'there's things on David's mind. I tried to explain to you at dinner but I didn't seem able to get it out. He's wondering why you've avoided Maoris in the past. Now's the time, I'm sure, to tell him the whole truth.'

Bob frowned, but recovered quickly, laughed loudly and said, 'Later. Don't let's spoil today. Let's just say I did have good reason not to want to get over-involved. All right, David?'

David took a deep breath. 'I know,' he said clearly and fearlessly. 'At least I've guessed one reason. My real father being Maori, in Auckland. I know that.'

David turned and ran. It was Bob's defeat he could not face, or his mother's emotion. He ran up to the shelter belt, jumped the fence and veered left towards the road away from the beach. He did not want them following him down there, and finding his grandfather. Not yet. From the shoulder of the hill he looked down. Bob had turned away, an arm round his wife. But she was looking back at David.

David hurried on. It had just occurred to him that, as Old Tama's only grandson, he had a serious duty to perform. He must put his courage to one more test. He must go back to Papanui, back to where long ago his ancestor, Tama, had died: and he must find the patu and clear up the Oha for once and for all.

12

At last David was sitting halfway up the Papanui headland
above the seal colony. Somewhere here Tama had been
hurled over the cliff. David wondered if his body had
been sucked out to sea or whether the Kati Mamoe had
found it – even perhaps eaten it. No funeral chant for
Tama. David remembered Hemi chanting that day down
on the beach. Some of the words were lodged in his mind.
'Stand up. Weep for us.'

David stood up. He found he could not weep for Tama
but the evening wind had changed quarter and made his
eyes water as it whipped at him from the south. The
weather forecast had been right after all. Clouds scudded
across the darkening sky. 'Look up to the mountain,'
Hemi had sung. 'Take the long path.'

David crawled to the uneven edge of the headland and
looked over. Leading across the crumbling yellow face of
the cliff he saw the faint thread of animal tracks. A little
wavering path. A little long path.

The track led to a ledge further down and on this lay the
dead sheep he had noticed the other day from the beach
below. How long had those cliffs held up that ledge?
David remembered the dream. Tama had thrown out his
hands as he fell. The patu would have dropped from his
outstretched fingers. Could it have slithered, like the dead
sheep, down to that ledge?

David knew it was Rawiri's duty to climb down and

search. Secure within his newfound courage he took off his shoes and began to follow the faint trail across the cracked yellow cliffs. Earth and pebbles slithered under his weight. Soon he had to sit on his heels and scuff his way steeply downwards. He dislodged a large stone, which dislodged others. They gathered speed and eventually crashed on to the boulders below. David heard the distant grunts and barks from startled seals. But he did not look down. He found a place where he could sit reasonably securely, then stretched out both legs and felt with his toes for a foothold. He bent his knees, edging his weight forwards on to his seat. Then he sat down again and stretched forward for another foothold. The gulls were wheeling round him, shrieking warnings. Or perhaps they were waiting for more carrion.

He was not very far away from the ledge, but now the 'long path' ended. The cliff was overhanging where there had been a slip. It was here that the sheep had lost its footing.

'Turn and take one more look –' David peered down. Below the path, level with the ledge where the sheep lay, was a horizontal crack in the cliff face like the crevices he had noticed from the beach. It was a very narrow slit. Resolutely David turned on to his stomach, found fingerholds for both hands and tried to let himself down to the ledge. He was surely tall enough to touch it with his toes –

But he was not. He was suddenly swinging by his fingernails, his feet in mid-air.

'The ledge *is* there,' David told himself, 'so here I come,' and he began sliding down fast. His feet landed on the edge but the speed of his descent threw him outwards. David grabbed and his fingers caught in the wool and bones of the dead sheep. He managed to hurl his weight inwards and stay sprawled on the ledge.

The sheep did not smell. It was past that. David lay on it gratefully for a few moments. Then he sat up, turned and knelt on the flattened carcase. Jumbled bones stuck out of the sandy shroud. David picked up a rib and levered up a flap of stiffened skin and fleece. Under it, at the back of the ledge, ran the crack in the cliff, the narrow slit. David dug into it, scuffling out the earth. He was not in any doubt. This was the right place. He probed with his fingers.

For a moment, a hundred metres below, he caught sight of the rocks and sea. Calmly he focused his eyes back on to his own hands. There was certainly something smooth and hard at his fingertips. David dug and scratched, first with one rib, then another. His excavations slowly revealed something pale. Evenly shaped. An artifact of some kind. A handle with a hole drilled in it. He loosened the earth all round, then at last laid hold of this handle and pulled.

Smoothly, like a lamb being born, the patu emerged. The whalebone patu. It lay in his hands, cold from its long entombment in the cliff, but intact, flawless, beautiful. Tarewai's whalebone patu. David found he was trembling. It was with great difficulty that he managed to get his fishing line out of his pocket and thread one end through the hole in the patu handle. The original flax string had rotted away. Making a loop, he hung the patu round his neck and tucked it under his shirt. Now all he had to do was to climb up the cliff and take the family heirloom back to his grandfather.

That was all he had to do. But the first two metres of the climb were a problem. He had slithered down: if only he could have slithered up too. David's mind seemed to rush up and down the maze of this problem. He came at last to the centre of it. Mountaineers had, well, pegs of a kind which they knocked into rock faces as footholds, and he had – sheep bones.

He collected the strongest leg bones, and using the end of one femur as a hammer, banged three other leg bones into the yielding yellow cliff. It was almost too easy, the clay too soft. But he thumped until only a few centimetres protruded. Those should hold just long enough for him to scramble up the overhang on to the track. He thrust a handful of spindly ribs into his back pocket, touched the patu as though it could bring him luck, then he climbed up his bone staircase.

Each bone yielded under his weight, but he was off it before it could give way. He got one knee on to the path, and suddenly the path itself started to crumble. David felt himself beginning to slide with it. In a flash he grabbed a rib from his back pocket and with all his might swung the hooked end into the cliff above, like a mountaineer trying to save himself with his ice axe. The rib caught in the clay, held only for a couple of seconds, but in that time David brought up his other knee and was scrambling on all fours along the upper section of the path as the lower part rumbled down the cliff face. He could hear the sea down below, hungry lips smacking and licking the boulders. He looked up and dark clouds were scudding by from the south so fast that for a moment he had the illusion that he was falling out from the cliff, flying like Tama into nothingness. Then he found grass under his fingers, saw a clover blossom. He was on level pasture. He was safe. But he went on crawling on hands and knees until he was a long way from the edge of the cliff.

For a few moments he lay still, thankful. Then he sat up and drew out the patu, rubbed it across his shirt. As he ran his finger down the edge, rain swept hissing over the headland.

Now it was a matter of getting home. David turned his back on the bite of the wind and rain and took off at a steady trot. It had not rained since the day of Abel's death, and now it came down in torrents. The grass was so dry that the raindrops ran off each blade and lay on the ground instead of soaking into the baked earth. Sheep sheltered on the lee side of the dry-stone walls.

David was soon soaked to the bone. With every step he could feel the patu jig against his chest. All the way he imagined in his head what would happen when he gave the patu to Old Tama, greeted him as 'Grandfather' for the first time. In his mind's eye he pictured the old man holding out his arms in welcome as he emerged from the back of the cave. Then he decided that in this weather Old Tama would more likely be at the cottage. He imagined the old man stirring his evening meal in a billy, over a drift-wood fire; the candles flickering – or more likely an old-fashioned oil lamp – as David opened the door and said –

David jogged through the storm, happier than he had ever been before. By the time he reached the beach below Penguin Pass the tide was coming in, each wave was an explosion. He lolloped along the sands. As he ran, another boy ran upside-down beneath him, blotchily reflected in the wet sand. David stopped to peer at the reflection. The boy peering back at him looked dark in the confused light, more like Tama than David.

David began to climb up the boulders near the foot of

the swollen creek. Lemon's chicks had taken shelter in the flax. David passed by only glancing at them, soggy feather dusters among the leaves, black and white feet like galoshes. It was getting too dark to distinguish the Blue family properly. The creek roared, bubbling and churning. It had flooded where fallen branches and silt half-blocked the watercourse and found a dozen different routes downhill.

Now that dusk was falling the rain had eased off. David managed to find the track to the cottage. The gorse had been beaten about by the storm, there were prickles in all directions. He pushed past. By the dry-stone wall and the hedge he hesitated. A last gust of wind blew in from the ocean, rattling the branches, clattering a loose sheet of corrugated iron. Then, except for the background roar of the creek and the booming of the breakers, the place seemed suddenly quiet. He could hear the sound of steady dripping somewhere nearby.

David picked his way past the coil of wire and with one hand pressing the patu to his chest he walked up to the cottage and mounted the rickety steps to the verandah.

'Grandfather!' he called.

The place looked totally deserted. But David thought he knew why. Old Tama had taken great care not to have his presence discovered too soon by Bob. That was why no light showed through the front window. There would be a fire and a lamp in the old kitchen round the back, where the windows were boarded up.

David took a step towards the front room, intending to tap. A plank in the verandah gave way and David's leg went right through to the ground below. 'Gee!' he thought, 'lucky Grandfather didn't do that! At his age.'

He extricated himself and walked round the house past the kennel to the lean-to porch by the back door. Here he had another surprise. The doorway itself was blocked by several cardboard boxes. David touched one and it rattled. He groped inside the top box. Traps. Lots of rabbit traps.

He knocked loudly on the door.

And again.

Something was terribly wrong. He tried the door handle and it turned. He shifted the boxes and then the door swung outwards, creaking. David stepped into the evil-smelling darkness inside.

'Grandfather!' he called. 'Old Tama! You all right?'

He stepped on something small which crunched under his foot. Bending down and putting out a hand, he felt around, and found it was exactly what he needed. A box of matches. He was shivering. His fingers were clumsy and the matches damp, but the fourth one lit. He held it up and looked round.

A deserted kitchen. As the match guttered he saw a bottle with a candle stuck in it on the window sill.

He shuffled in that direction. His fingers brushed through the thick dust on the ledge and touched the bottle. It took ten damp matches before he could light the candle.

There was nothing in the kitchen except a rusty wood range and a sink. And rat droppings all over the floor.

'Grandfather!' he called again. But not very loudly. Anyone could tell the house was empty.

In spite of that David began to search, holding the bottle with the candle in his left hand. He peered through a door on his right. Nothing at all. Another door opened out of the kitchen into the front passage. He could see the sky through the fanlight over the front door. He peered into the room on his right. Through a hole in the ceiling rainwater dripped from a leaking roof on to a heap of plaster and rubble in the middle of the floor and on to the frame of a large bedstead. David put out a finger and touched the iron. Inches of dust peeled off and floated to the floor.

The room on the left had two windows, one boarded up. The other was the window where David had once detected a movement. As he stepped forwards there was a scuffle from in front of him, below him. He raised the candle. The floor boards had rotted away, only the main joists remained. And from its home among the rotten planks a possum – or was it a polecat? – anyway a pair of eyes reflected the gleam of candlelight.

David turned away and walked back through the kitchen to the back door. Just before the candle was blown out by the draught, he saw the name *WAKA* scribbled across one of the boxes of traps stowed under the porch.

David put down the bottle, pushed his way outside. His teeth were chattering and he was cold, icily cold, not only his body but his spirit. No Old Tama. No one had stayed at the cottage. Henare used it as a base for his possibly illicit trapping activities and knew the whole building was unsafe.

David pulled the patu out from under his shirt and stroked it lovingly. The patu was real. The Oha was accomplished. That was all true.

13

In the fast-falling dark David was scrambling back through the prickles of the gorse path. He had to go to the cave. Now he was suddenly caught up by the rushing waters of the creek. He braced himself against the current and emerged on the path below the cave without finding any of the submerged stepping-stones.

Now he scrambled up the slippery bank towards the silent barrier. But this time there was no silence. Instead there was a rumble from up the hillside and the creek kept up an incessant roar. David found he was standing on the threshold of the cave and his last shred of hope had vanished. He knew that Old Tama would never be there again. Hemi had spoken the truth about returned spirits. 'You'd never guess,' he had said, 'except for certain things.' Well, David had noticed certain things and ignored them.

'A knot in the grass,' thought David. 'He tied one because of me. He came all the way back to find me and pass on the family Oha.'

And now, his task accomplished, Old Tama had quietly

disappeared. By now he would be back in the house of the ancestors, with his son, who needed him. 'Haere ra! Haere ra! Farewell, Old Tama,' cried Rawiri, his grandson.

David knelt down. The patu swung out on its string and brushed his knees. He groped around, searching for Mabel and the chick. His fingers touched the sticky nest-site, but it was empty.

'Mabel!'

He crawled towards the back of the cave where the ground was dry and a trench, together with piles of earth, bore proof of the reality of Old Tama's digging. His fingers brushed against the thick down of Mabel's chick who was sheltering out of the wet.

'You've got some sense, Young Abel,' whispered David. 'You're going to turn out just like your father even if you don't remember him.'

It occurred to David that in several ways he had a lot in common with Young Abel.

Suddenly from up the hillside there came another rumbling roar as loose rocks began crashing downhill. Cracks in the parched ground had filled with rain and now the topsoil was slipping like an avalanche of mud.

David clutched at the chick and crouched at the back of the cave in Old Tama's trench. Now the main slip was over and a few last stones pattered downhill. Branches creaked and snapped under the weight of loose earth. David and the chick were unharmed, protected by the trench and the overhang; but they were imprisoned by the rubble that blocked the entrance to the cave.

The chick was used to being touched. It allowed David to pick it up and rub his chin against its warm down, which felt like a cosy winter dressing-gown. Its dumpy body exuded the same sort of comfort as a familiar teddy-bear.

'Don't be scared,' said David, to reassure himself rather than the chick. 'I'll soon get us out of here.' He extended his legs, but withdrew them hastily as more stones cascaded down.

'Seems we'll just have to sit it out together,' he said. 'My Mum'll notice I'm not home. And my stepfather, he'll search all night if he has to. He's not the kind to give in.' It was almost a boast. 'What about your mother, Young Abel? When does she get back? What time's your dinner? About now, surely?'

It was then, right on cue, that they both heard a slithering sound and a pat-pat of irresolute footsteps. The chick, which had been lying quietly in David's arms, began to wriggle and peck. 'There she is now,' exclaimed David. 'Smack on time.'

'Mabel!' he called. 'Fetch help! Take a message. Do something clever. We're relying on you.'

Mabel had just the one thought in her yellow head, which was to feed her chick. She was to be heard paddling back and forth searching for a way to her nest which was now under the landslip.

'I suppose you'd better go,' sighed David to Young Abel. 'No need for us both to go hungry. You'll wriggle out somehow.'

He unclasped his fingers; then suddenly he clenched them shut again. 'No!' he cried. The chick floundered and squeaked. Mabel made crooning, gobbling, feeding noises to encourage it. As David tightened his grip the chick kicked and fought.

'Sorry about this,' said David grimly, squeezing a little tighter, 'but you'll survive.'

Now the chick was in a panic, swearing and squeaking. Mabel was acutely distressed. David could hear her big feet stamping and trampling in the mud. For the second time in her life she was confronted by a situation which was too much for her. For several minutes she hesitated on the edge of panic. Her bill began to stutter and clack, and then it came, the penguin call of despair, the cry which David had heard once before at dawn when Abel died. Shriek followed shriek, an agonized crescendo of trident screams.

And that was why, ten minutes later, David heard more floundering footsteps tripping and slithering in the mud. Joy, as she had once promised, was answering the penguin cry for help. In her husband's big gumboots she tumbled and squelched to the rescue.

'I'm here, Mum,' called David. 'I'm all right. Everything's all right now.'

'Off you go, Young Abel,' he said as the chick helter-skeltered out through the gap to Mabel. And he smiled, fingering the patu, as he listened to the approach of his own flustered but undaunted mother.

Glossary of Maori words

Haere mai Welcome

Haere ra koe Farewell to you

Ka kite ano See you again

Karakia Incantation

Kia ora Hello

Mana (To lose mana) Standing (To lose face)

Marae Grass area in front of meeting-house where matters are discussed

Mere pounamu Greenstone club

Oha Last wishes of someone who is dying

Pa Fortified village

Pakeha New Zealander of European descent

Patu paraoa Whalebone club

Poi Ball on end of string twirled by Maori women when dancing

Tangi Funeral ritual

Tapu Sacred; a restricted or forbidden area

Tohunga Maori expert; priest

Po kare kare ana Nga wai o Rotorua   Rippling are the waters of Rotorua

E hine e   My love
Hoki mai ra   Come back to me

Ka mate ahau i   Or I will die
Te aroha e   For (the) love of you

Author's Note

I am indebted to many people for advice in writing thi
book, though none of them can be held responsible fo
the final result.

In particular I would like to thank my husband for hi
loyal co-operation and encouragement. Also Mur
Walters for his help with the Maori language, Stuar
Park of Auckland Museum, and the staff of the Hocke
Library, Dunedin. I am indebted to *The Maoris of th
South Island* by T.A. Pybus and *Maori Death Customs* b
R.S. Openheim for source material on Tarewai and th
'Oha'.

I must also thank the Yellow-Eyed Penguins whos
private lives I have studied and recorded.

Joan de Ham